A
CINDERELLA
STORY

D0962903

A CINDERELLA STORY

Adapted by Robin Wasserman
Based on a screenplay by Leigh Dunlap

SCHOLASTIC INC.

New York   Toronto   London   Auckland   Sydney
Mexico City   New Delhi   Hong Kong   Buenos Aires

If you purchased this book without a cover, you should be aware that this book is stolen property. It was reported as "unsold and destroyed" to the publisher, and neither the author nor the publisher has received any payment for this "stripped book."

No part of this publication may be reproduced in whole or in part, or stored in a retrieval system, or transmitted in any form or by any means, electronic, mechanical, photocopying, recording, or otherwise, without written permission of the publisher. For information regarding permission, write to Scholastic Inc., Attention: Permissions Department, 557 Broadway, New York, NY 10012.

ISBN 0-439-65341-X

Copyright © Warner Bros. Entertainment Inc.
SCHOLASTIC and associated logos are trademarks and/or registered trademarks of Scholastic Inc.

Designed by Louise Bova

12 11 10 9 8 7 6 5 4 3   4 5 6 7 8 9/0

Printed in the U.S.A.

First printing, July 2004

A
CINDERELLA
STORY

chapter one

*O*nce upon a time, in a faraway kingdom, lived a beautiful little girl and her widowed father.

Okay, so it wasn't really a faraway kingdom. It was LA's San Fernando Valley, a totally unmagical suburb of a totally unmagical city — and it only looked faraway because you could barely see it through all the smog. But for Samantha Montgomery, it was all the kingdom she needed — it was home.

Sure, sometimes Sam missed having a mom, but her father made sure she never missed out on anything. They were best friends, and they did everything together. Being raised by a guy might have put her behind in the makeup and fashion departments, but Sam didn't care about any of that stuff. She didn't want to play with dolls or have tea parties; she wanted to climb trees and ride bikes and play softball — and that's exactly what she did, with her dad right by her side. As Sam saw it, she was pretty much the luckiest girl in the world.

Life was perfect. Her dad owned Hal's Diner, the coziest, tastiest restaurant in the Valley, and for Sam, it was a home away from home. Everything about the place reminded her of her dad, especially the quote hanging over the front door. It read, NEVER LET THE FEAR OF STRIKING OUT KEEP YOU FROM PLAYING THE GAME, and even at seven years old, Sam knew what that meant. It meant that she should be fearless, that she should try her best, that she could be anything she wanted to be — and she knew she could do it, because her father would be there right beside her the whole way.

♕   ♕   ♕

And then, just when life seemed most perfect, everything changed.

It was Sam's eighth birthday, and it started out as the best day of her life. Hal's Diner was a place where everybody felt like family, and a birthday — especially an eighth birthday — was a big deal. Everyone was there: Eleanor and Rhonda, the waitresses; Bobby, the cook; Sam's best friend, Carter; and of course, her dad. They all squeezed around a table in the diner, and when Bobby brought out the cake and set it down in front of her, Sam was so happy, she thought her heart might explode.

"Make a wish, Princess," Rhonda told her with a wink. But Sam didn't know what to wish for — after all, it's hard to think of a good wish when you have everything you ever wanted. So she closed her eyes, because that's what you do when you're eight years old and you need to think really hard.

And since her eyes were closed, she never saw it coming.

"It," of course, meant "her."

Fiona.

Fiona, tall, thin, and beautiful — that is, if you like that disgustingly well manicured, every hair in its place and every eyebrow tweezed to perfection kind of look.

Fiona, perfectly composed — and perfectly horrible.

Fiona, who had never made a false move in her life, walked past the birthday party, tripped over her own two feet, and fell into Sam's father's arms — and into his life. As Sam blew out the candles, wishing only that her life would stay exactly as it was at that moment, she opened her eyes to grin up at her father, the one who'd made all this perfection possible. But her father wasn't looking at her, not anymore. He was looking at Fiona — *gazing* at Fiona. And that was that.

You can guess the rest. Love at first sight. Dinner. Dancing. Moonlit walks along the beach. Blah, blah, blah. And before you knew it — the storybook wedding. All it took was a few vows, two "I do's," a giant diamond ring — and Fiona was officially part of the family. For richer, for poorer, till death do us part, and all the rest.

It was enough to make you sick.

And believe it or not, that wasn't even the worst part.

Sam's new stepmother had been married five times before. Husband number two resulted in the birth of twins,

Brianna and Gabriella . . . Sam's new stepsisters. *This* was a family picture that Sam did *not* want to be a part of.

But no one had asked her. And now there they were, one big happy family . . . not.

Even so, years later when Sam looked back on those days, she realized that things weren't quite as bad as they seemed. Sure, Fiona was a hideous excuse for a step-mother, and Brianna and Gabriella, well, they barely qualified as human, much less as sisters. They certainly weren't anyone that Sam wanted to share her house with. But at least she still *had* her house, and it was still — despite the unwelcome permanent guests — perfect. She still had her perfect room, her perfect diner, and, of course, her perfect dad.

She still had her fairy tale.

If only it had lasted just a little longer.

♕   ♕   ♕

When she was older, Sam always thought it was strange that she didn't remember much about that day, the day it happened. She didn't remember what she'd had for dinner, or what she was wearing, or who had won the softball game that afternoon.

But that night — that she remembered perfectly. Too perfectly. Sometimes, when she closed her eyes, she could still see him sitting next to her bed, reading out of their favorite book of fairy tales.

"And the beautiful Princess and her handsome Prince

rode off to his castle and lived happily ever after," he'd read. Then he closed the book and leaned over to kiss her good night.

"Do fairy tales come true, Dad?" Sam had asked.

Her father smiled. "No, but dreams come true," he told her. "If there's something you really want, if it's your dream, you can make it happen."

"Do you have a dream?" she asked.

"My dream is that you'll grow up, go to college, and maybe someday build your own castle," he said.

But Sam wasn't ready to go to bed, so she came up with another very important question. "Where do princesses go to college?"

She'd almost stumped him with that one, Sam remembered. He paused for a long moment, and then began, "Why, they go to . . . they go to this place where there's a . . ." He paused again, then grinned. "A place where there's a ton of young princes. Princeton."

"Should I go to Princeton?" Sam asked. She didn't actually know what Princeton was, but if her dad wanted her to go there, it sounded like a good idea. Plus, what princess wouldn't want to go to a land full of princes?

"Nothing would make me happier," her father said. "But Sam, fairy tales aren't just about meeting handsome princes." He gestured toward the fairy-tale book, from which they read a story every night. "They're about fulfilling dreams and standing up for what you believe in."

Sam looked confused (she was, after all, only eight years old).

"It's like I always say," her father continued, trying to help her understand. "Never let the fear of striking out . . ."

". . . keep you from playing the game!" Sam finished for him. She'd heard it a million times before, but it never got old.

Her father handed her the book of fairy tales. "Just remember," he told her, "if you look carefully, this book contains important things you may need to know later in life."

Sam nodded — he didn't need to tell her. She already knew that life was a fairy tale and that her favorite book had all the information she needed to get by in the world.

And then, before her father could tuck her in, her world began to fall apart. Literally. Her bed, her nightstand, her book, her entire house felt like it was shaking itself to pieces. And any Californian, even an eight-year-old, knew what that meant. Earthquake!

"Quick, under the doorway!" Sam cried, knowing that was the safest place to be until the quake ended. She grabbed her father's hand and they ran to the doorway, to safety.

Then they heard it. Fiona's voice.

"Help!" she shrieked. "My cat! My cat!"

Sam's father moved toward the hallway, but Sam clung to his hand.

"Don't go," she pleaded, pulling him toward her. But although she was holding him as tightly as she could, he pulled away, racing down the hall to rescue Fiona's darling pet.

"I'll be back," he promised Sam, who was hugging the doorway, tears streaming down her face.

And he disappeared down the hall.

Just like that, he was gone.

"I'll be back," he'd said.

It was the first time he'd ever broken a promise.

chapter two

*A*fter that, everything changed.

Sam's father — her best friend — was gone.

She was alone.

Everywhere she went, everything she did reminded her of him. The softball field, where he'd taught her to pitch. The diner, where they'd shared milk shakes and secrets. The house where she'd grown up, the house that reminded her so much of him, from his picture in the hall to the creaky stair he'd never gotten around to fixing, to the chair by her bed, where he'd read her one last bed-time story.

The house that wasn't hers any longer.

Sam's father hadn't left a will, which meant that Fiona got *everything* — the house, the diner, and, to her dismay, Sam. After about five minutes, Fiona snapped out of mourning and into action. She fixed all the earthquake damage, but didn't stop there. Not Fiona, fashion queen. She whipped out her catalogues, her cell phone, and her credit card, and in no time at all had turned the house into a disaster of tackiness that Sam barely recognized.

Her perfect bedroom was the first to go — and when

the renovations were complete, and the softball trophies had been replaced by something suitably pink and vomitous, Sam was forced out and Brianna moved on in.

It was only the beginning. With Sam's father out of the way, Fiona could finally show her true colors, and this wicked stepmother couldn't wait to get started. Sam got the worst of everything, starting with her new "bedroom," aka, the attic.

The attic may have been dark and dirty, filled with dust and cobwebs, but Sam didn't care — it was the room farthest away from Fiona and her evil offspring, so it was just fine with her. When she'd lugged her last box upstairs (certainly no one in the house was going to help her move, despite the fact that the box weighed more than she did), she sat down on her creaky cot and looked around her.

This is it, she thought grimly. *This is my life now.*

It was the end of a dream and the beginning of a nightmare.

chapter three

$\mathcal{T}$hat was eight years ago, and nothing had improved in the meantime. You don't need to hear the details to believe that — just imagine living life in an attic, surrounded by a stepfamily that just wishes you would disappear.

Some days were better, some days were worse, but in general, nothing much changed. Sam got older and older, her stepsisters got uglier and meaner, and Fiona got better and better at making Sam's life miserable.

But here's the thing: Sam was tough, and she made it through. She even made it bearable. Almost. She'd hidden the grimy walls of her attic bedroom behind a layer of posters, and filled the room with hundreds of books that she loved, books that had gotten her through so many long nights growing up. A Princeton banner reminded her that there was hope for the future — and her prized possession, a picture of her and her dad at their last Dodgers game together, reminded her that life hadn't always been this hard. Sometimes, shut up in her room, enjoying her privacy and dreaming of the future, she could almost forget the realities of her present. And then —

"Sa-a-a-a-a-a-a-m!" screamed Fiona. The wicked

stepmother herself, still around and still the bane of Sam's existence. Did she care that it was five A.M.? That Sam was sleeping? That the entire world didn't exist merely to serve her every whim?

Not a chance.

"Where's my salmon!" she called, her piercing voice flying up the stairs and rocketing Sam out of her sleep more efficiently than the loudest alarm clock. "I need my salmon!"

(Yes, you read that right, her *salmon* — just wait, you'll understand soon enough.)

♔   ♔   ♔

Sam carried the plate out into the backyard, ready to rescue Fiona from her salmon crisis. The sun was still hovering on the horizon, but she knew Fiona would already be lounging by the pool, watching her two precious daughters practice their synchronized swimming.

Brianna and Gabriella, wearing matching bathing suits, swim caps, and nose plugs, were performing mirror exercises in the shimmering water under the watchful eye of their synchronized-swimming coach, Blaine.

Blaine was a man in his mid-thirties who spent his days teaching prissy suburban girls how to spin around in the water at the same time. And that's about all you need to know about him.

"Come on, girls," he called to them, "let's keep our concentration. You're a mirror of each other."

Brianna — or maybe Gabriella — seemed confused. "Is that me? Or is that my reflection?"

Sam shook her head, trying not to laugh. Apparently the complicated concepts involved in this "sport" were a little too much for her idiot stepsisters.

"Sam!" Fiona shouted, distracting her from her morning's amusement.

"Coming," she said, and — slowly as humanly possible — made her way over to Fiona's lounge chair. Fiona looked pretty much as she had eight years before, although she'd expanded about two dress sizes since then (refusing to admit that, she continued to buy clothes appropriate for a woman half her size). Sam winced, thinking that she was almost related to this . . . this *creature* — badly chosen clothes, badly colored hair, badly done nose job, and all.

This morning, as every morning this month, Fiona had her favorite new book propped open in front of her: *The Salmon Diet*. Sam wasn't sure Fiona had actually *read* the book (actually, Sam wasn't too sure that Fiona could read at all), but the woman had certainly taken it to heart. This was only the latest in a long string of fad diets Fiona had picked up and dropped over the years. None of them seemed to work . . . but they did provide Sam with an endless source of entertainment.

"Is this the Norwegian salmon?" Fiona asked. "I need my Omega-threes."

Her what? But Sam just smiled politely and nodded. "They're Norwegian salmon, just like you asked."

"They better be," Fiona said, shooting her a warning look. Then she glanced over at the pool, where Brianna and Gabriella were attempting an elaborately symbolic water dance — either that or they were trying to drown each other. "Just look at them," Fiona continued, her voice dripping with poisonous motherly warmth. "So, so, so, so gifted."

Sam looked again and stifled a laugh — yes, definitely trying to drown each other.

"Well, don't just stand there with your mouth gaping open!" Fiona snapped. "Get to work!"

"But I have school," Sam protested.

Fiona looked disgusted. "Oh, school, schmool," she said. "Stop being such a whiner. Most kids would love to skip school." She waved her hand — the signal that Sam and her mundane concerns were officially dismissed. "Now get going!"

Sam sighed and traipsed back toward the house. If she was going to head over to the diner this morning, she might as well get it over with. And then, just when it seemed like the morning couldn't get off to a worse start, the sprinklers went off. Right where Sam was standing.

Drenched, Sam raced for the spigot to turn off the water.

"Leave them!" Fiona commanded. "The lawn is looking a little brown."

"But we're supposed to be conserving," Sam reminded her. The state of California was in a drought crisis (though really, when wasn't it?), and lawn sprinklers were definitely on the list of "don't's."

"But we're supposed to be conserving," Fiona mimicked her in a baby's voice. She looked at Sam as if her stepdaughter was a wet and bedraggled stray dog who'd just stumbled onto the property — and was destined for the pound. "Droughts are for poor people. You think Madonna has a brown lawn? We have class." And with that, Fiona stuffed an enormous piece of salmon into her mouth and went back to "reading" her book.

Sam shook her head, heading back into the house. That was Fiona in a nutshell. Always thinking of those less fortunate than herself — thinking of them and then, of course, shrugging in indifference.

chapter four

Sam tossed her books into the car and took off for the diner. Her dad's old convertible had seen better days, but it did the job — and it still reminded her of him.

Which was more than she could say for the diner.

Sam still shuddered every time she saw it, her beautiful old diner redone Fiona-style, complete with a giant neon sign (reading "Fiona's," of course) and an Elvis-shaped clock covering up her dad's favorite quote. That Fiona, she was a real class act.

The inside was even worse — but at least Sam's surrogate family was still around. Sam smiled, watching Rhonda and Bobby fight in the kitchen as they always did, like an old married couple.

"Bobby, that's enough with the salmon," Rhonda complained. "Salmon omelets, salmon soup, salmon pudding. We're gonna grow gills!"

Bobby didn't look any happier with the salmon than Rhonda did, but he knew his job. "Rhonda, those are Fiona's favorites," he reminded her.

As Rhonda came out of the kitchen and began chatting up the customers, Sam ducked into the back to change into her uniform. Vintage 1950s-era "Fiona's Diner" shirt, 1950s-era "Fiona's Diner" skirt, and — though she still couldn't believe that such a humiliating possibility had actually come to pass — 1950s-era "Fiona's Diner" *roller skates*. What a job. What a life.

The morning passed as it always did — Sam bussed her tables, tried not to topple off her skates, and did her best to leaf through the occasional textbook as she rolled by. She usually tried to strategically position her homework throughout the diner so that she would at least have a chance to get part of it done. Sam assumed that Princeton wasn't really in the market for a roller-skating waitress who had flunked out of high school, so she was doing her best to make sure it didn't come to that. So far, so good.

"Sam, what are you still doing here?" Rhonda asked.

"I'm almost done," Sam called back over her shoulder as she rolled on to her next stack of dirty dishes.

"You're going to be late for school," Rhonda warned.

"I'll get there. Fiona goes ballistic if I don't finish."

Rhonda balled up her fists in frustration. "I couldn't care less about Fiona," she bellowed. "What I care about is your education."

"But . . ."

"Getting up at the crack of dawn like some kind of rooster," Rhonda complained.

"But . . ."

"Your dad would want you at school, not here."

"But . . ."

"That's enough buts," Rhonda cut her off. "You just leave Fiona and her big butt to me."

Sam had to laugh. "Thanks, Rhonda," she said, giving her friend a hug. She grabbed her books and was about to run out of the diner when she remembered — her '50s clothes. Her '50s skates. Her totally not-'50s school.

Better change first.

♛   ♛   ♛

Sam pulled up to Carter's house, hoping he hadn't been waiting too long.

Carter was her best friend, and had been since she was a kid. He had never cared that she was a total tomboy and she had never cared that he was totally . . . weird.

Who knows, maybe that's why they got along so well.

When Sam arrived, Carter's father was out in the driveway, intently bent over the tire of his convertible with a toothbrush and a can of Armor All.

"Looking good, Mr. Farrell," Sam called out the window.

"A man's best friend is his Mercedes, Sam," Mr. Farrell said. As he said every time she saw him. They were words he most definitely lived by.

"I'll remember that," Sam said, suppressing a smile.

Before she could learn any more about the joys of owning, driving, polishing, and generally loving a Mercedes,

Carter strolled out of the house and down the driveway to join them. He was dressed like a pimp. From the 1970s.

"*Anything* is possible, if you just believe," he greeted them.

It's probably important to note here that Carter was an actor. Wannabe actor, at least. Now, in most cities, if you were sixteen years old and you wanted to be an actor, you would try out for some school plays, maybe watch a lot of movies, and basically spend your high school years hanging with the drama crowd and dreaming of the future. But this was LA, baby (as they say). And as far as Carter was concerned, the future was too long to wait. He didn't want to be an actor when he grew up, he wanted to be one yesterday. And, were you to ask him, he would tell you he already *was* an actor — he was just waiting for the world to notice.

"Audition today?" his father asked. Hmm, how'd he guess?

"Five o'clock," Carter answered, holding up a script page. "I have one line." He squinted down at the page. "Anything *is* possible, if you just believe."

Sure, it was just a line, but Carter believed it. The boy was an incurable optimist — but Sam tried not to hold it against him.

Carter waved hello to Sam and pulled open the passenger-side door. He hesitated before getting in, wrinkling his nose in disgust at the decrepit interior and the door, which looked as if one wrong move might knock it off its hinges.

"See what you force me to drive to school in, Dad?" Carter asked. "No offense, Sam," he added over his shoulder. "Don't you feel bad for me?"

"No," his father said. "I feel bad about the three cars you totaled."

"You are so overreacting," Carter complained. "I just had a run of bad luck."

"It takes more than bad luck to drive a car into Lake Castaic. That takes skill and planning."

Carter sighed. His father had a point. He hated it when that happened. He hopped into the car and slammed the door behind him.

"What are you wearing?" Sam asked, catching her first up-close look at Carter's bizarro outfit.

"It's my Snoop Dogg look," he said.

Sam turned off the ignition. "I'm not driving you to school like that," she said firmly.

"Oh, come on," Carter whined. "I'm a method actor. This is my training."

The car stayed off.

Carter sighed again — totally defeated, twice in the space of five minutes. He opened the car door and slunk back toward his house to change. "There goes my Oscar."

chapter five

$\mathcal{T}$he old car chugged into the school lot, and Sam and Carter began the painful daily ritual of searching for a parking space. It seemed to be one of the rules of high school that the parking lot was structured like a particularly frustrating game of musical chairs, inevitably containing fewer spaces than there were cars. Typical high school mind games.

"Primo parking spot dead ahead," Carter crowed, pointing through the windshield.

Sam carefully pulled forward toward the space. But just as she was about to pull into it . . . cut off!

A vintage Thunderbird veered ahead of her and swung into the empty spot. Noticing Sam's irritation, the three girls in the car laughed and high-fived one another. "You snooze, you lose," they sang out in sync.

Meet Shelby, Madison, and Caitlyn.

Shelby Cummings ruled the school — or at least, thought she did (and had most of the student body pretty much convinced). She also ruled Madison and Caitlyn, who would have done anything to stay in their queen's good favor. Shelby — and, because she told them to,

Madison and Caitlyn — always dressed in the latest styles, kept her hair perfectly groomed and her nails impeccably manicured. Sam thought they were ridiculous. Carter thought they were a little piece of heaven.

"Well, if it isn't Shelby Cummings and her posse," Carter swooned, gazing at the love of his life. "Shelby wants me so bad."

"You've never even talked to her," Sam reminded him scornfully.

"I've talked to her," Carter protested. "At least . . . in my mind. And let me tell you . . . in my mind, she wants me oh so bad."

"Carter, you can do so much better than Shelby Cummings," Sam said. "Even in your mind." She would never understand Carter's obsession with this girl. She just hoped it would pass, and soon.

"Hey, there's another spot," Carter observed, gesturing off to the side.

Sam turned her car and aimed it toward the new spot. And, just as she was about to pull into it, her car stalled!

"Oh, come on!" Sam cried, pounding the steering wheel in frustration.

And at that instant, a Freelander came out of nowhere, swooped in, and stole the space. "You snooze, you lose!" the Freelander boys called out.

The doors opened and the space thieves piled out, slapping hands.

Meet Austin, Ryan, and David — Shelby and Co.'s male counterparts. From his silky, golden brown hair, to his intense eyes, to his perfectly chiseled body, Austin was almost a work of art — and of course, it didn't hurt that he was captain of the football team, president of the student body, and effortlessly, impossibly charming. Half the school was in love with Austin Ames, and he knew it. If the guys were a boy band, Austin would definitely have been Justin Timberlake — and Ryan and David stuck around as his backup singers in hopes that they might land some of his leftover groupies. Austin didn't need them — he had Shelby. (Who else would be good enough for the king of the school?)

"Austin!" she called, wiggling a finely manicured hand in his direction.

"We've got a serious crisis on our hands," she informed him as she approached, Madison and Caitlyn following close behind.

"What's wrong?" Austin asked.

"Now, the way I see things, we have a lock on the senior poll for best couple, best bods, best smiles, and most popular," Shelby explained. "But we're lagging behind in class humanitarians, so I was thinking we should do something involving humanity."

Austin looked surprised, then thoughtful. "Not a bad idea," he said. "There's this big-brother program downtown that we —"

"No, no, no, no, no," Shelby interrupted, shivering at the thought of interacting with the masses. The horror of it! What was he thinking? "I just meant we should write some checks to . . . I don't know, like, the whales? People love it when you save them."

Austin shook his head. "You're all heart, Shelby."

"I am, Austin," she defended herself.

Sam, watching — okay, eavesdropping on — the whole encounter, couldn't believe her eyes and ears.

"People like Austin and Shelby are genetically programmed to find each other," she said incredulously. "How can that much ego be in one relationship?"

"Imagine what they say about you," Carter pointed out.

Sam laughed. "They don't even know I exist."

And that's when Shelby noticed them staring.

"Oh, pyew," she said, wrinkling her nose. "Stalker-azzi at three o'clock."

Madison and Caitlyn knew their role, and they played it to perfection.

"Hey, diner doofus, can I get some waffles to go?" Madison asked.

"Nice Granny-mobile," Caitlyn added, shooting a sarcastic glance down at the convertible.

Shelby grabbed Madison's cheerleader megaphone and aimed it at Sam. "This zone is for cool people only," she boomed. "No geeks!"

The A-list ladies laughed and walked off.

Carter turned toward Sam with a self-satisfied smile. "And you thought they didn't know you existed."

♛   ♛   ♛

Sam and Carter pushed their way through the throng of students flooding into the school; like the parking lot, the front doors always seemed — almost deliberately — just too small to accommodate all the people pressing through them. High schools could be so sadistic sometimes.

They headed toward their lockers, rolling their eyes as Astrid, the school DJ (don't forget, this *is* LA), began her daily monologue. Their lockers were right next to the DJ booth, and Astrid peered out through the glass as they walked by. Checking out Carter? Was it possible? Captain Oblivious, of course, never noticed — he was still imagining the way Shelby's face would look on the day she declared her love for him.

"*Buenos dias,* Fighting Frogs! Here's your daily drought reminder to conserve *agua*," Astrid announced in an artificially cheery voice that totally belied her personality. Astrid was actually prettier than most of the popular girls, like Shelby and her crew, but she refused to have anything to do with that crowd. Hiding behind her dark makeup and an even darker view of the world, she preferred to stand on the sidelines and mock.

Sam loved her.

But she could never understand why Astrid would want to serve as the voice of the school, mouthing administration policies she didn't agree with and advertising events that — under normal circumstances — she wouldn't be caught dead attending.

"And don't forget," Astrid continued, "today's your last day to pick up tickets to the big Homecoming Halloween Dance. Whoop-ditty-doo! You too can dress up like someone you're not, for a change. I mean, let's get real."

Sam burst into laughter — there was the Astrid she knew and loved. She turned around to wave hello, just in time to see Mrs. Wells — a stickler for doing things the "proper" way in her classroom and in the world at large — rapping on the DJ booth window.

"Just stick to the announcements, Astrid," she yelled through the glass.

Astrid sighed. "I pledge allegiance to the flag," she began, as Mrs. Wells stood up stick-straight and proudly held her hand over her heart. Now, *this* was the proper way to begin the morning . . .

♛   ♛   ♛

Shelby, Madison, and Caitlyn, of course, didn't need to push through crowds. Girls like that don't push, they glide.

As the student body jumped out of their way, Shelby and her girls swept through the hall like royalty, brushing away their subjects with a decisively uttered "Move," whenever any of the masses came too close to touching them.

Brianna and Gabriella, never too quick on the uptake, hadn't gotten the memo that they weren't supposed to speak to Her Royal Highness and her ladies in waiting.

They waved as the clique passed by, like eager puppy dogs wagging their tails. Only not cute.

"Shelby, hey, Sister-Friend!" Gabriella tossed out.

Shelby shot her a phony smile — one that didn't even begin to melt the ice in her eyes — then turned back to her friends.

"Remind me again why we tolerate them?" she whined.

"Because they gave you a Prada bag for your birth-day," Madison suggested.

Caitlyn snorted — in a ladylike way, of course. "Try Fraud-a-bag. Totally fake."

"Oh yeah." Shelby made a mental note. Her brain may not have been her best asset, but it had plenty of space for a daily update to the list of who was hot and who was most definitely *not*.

Onward and upward. The procession continued, the girls moving and speaking as one.

"Move . . . move . . . move . . ."

Sam watched in disgust. It was hard for her to decide who was more pathetic here — Shelby, for thinking she ruled the world, or Brianna and Gabriella, for believing her. But before she could pick a winner, her very own stalker startled her out of her reverie.

"Greetings, Samantha," Terry said, sidling up beside her as he did every morning. "You look absolutely stunning today, as per usual."

Sam forced a smile. "Thanks, Terry." Terry looked as per his usual, too — though Sam noticed he was wearing his favorite T-shirt, which announced to the world that "Darth Vader Was Framed." Sam knew that Terry believed it with all his heart.

If Shelby and Austin perched on the top rung of the high school social ladder and Sam and Carter were stuck at the bottom, then Terry, well . . . Terry didn't even know the ladder existed. Terry thought he was on an escalator. On a completely different planet.

"Terry is my Earth name," he reminded her. "I prefer to be known by the name betrothed to me by my extraterrestrial brethren."

Well, this was even better than usual. "What is it?" Sam asked.

"It's a high-pitched squeal, dangerous to the fragile ears of earthlings," he explained. "Therefore, I cannot tell you." Terry's watch beeped, and he looked down at it, alarmed. "If you'll excuse me, I must get back to my galaxy now," he said quickly, and rushed away.

Carter chuckled softly. "Poor guy."

"Hey, at least he's happy," Sam pointed out.

"Happy?" Carter repeated incredulously. "He lives in another world!'"

"He's not alone," Sam said, looking down at the ground. "Sometimes fantasy is better than reality."

Before Carter could ask her what was going on with her — and he knew it was something — Sam's cell phone rang. She whipped it out, smiling at the words 1 TEXT MESSAGE blinking on the screen.

"Speaking of fantasy . . ." Carter said knowingly as Sam took off down the hall, beaming.

"I'll catch you later!" she called back over her shoulder.

Carter shook his head, bemused. "The secret admirer beckons."

♛   ♛   ♛

Yes, one more thing you need to know about Sam: She had a secret admirer. Or, rather, a secret pen pal. It was just a little thing, but it was also the one thing that made her life bearable these days.

It just happened to be a little . . . embarrassing. After all, what does it say about you when the highlight of your

daily social life is an electronic conversation with someone you've never met?

For all Sam knew, Mr. Right could turn out to be Terry.
But she hoped not — because to her, he seemed more like
Prince Charming.

Sam raced into the courtyard and slouched down
next to her favorite tree, reading her text message.

**Where have u been? We haven't talked in
ages.**

We talked this morning, Sam wrote, hitting
SEND. A moment later, her cell phone vibrated.

I can't stop thinking about u, she read. Wow.
What to say to that?

What's on your mind right now? he continued.

You first, she typed playfully.

**I'm thinking Professor Rothman's dis-
sected one 2 many frogs.**

Sam looked up just in time to see Professor Rothman
walking across the courtyard with a definite hop in his
step — his shirt, tie, and suit were all a very froggy green.

Sam's phone vibrated again, and she looked down to
read: **It's Kermit's Revenge.**

Sam laughed — then gasped as something occurred
to her. Was he out there somewhere? Seeing the same
things she was seeing? Seeing *her*?

She scanned the courtyard, looking for a familiar

face — not that it would necessarily be familiar. There weren't too many people outside this early in the day, but she spotted a few:

A wannabe rapper typing away on his cell phone and bopping to an imagined beat.

A wannabe beatnik, typing away on his cell phone — probably composing a deep new poem. She hoped.

Terry, techno-stalker, typing away on *his* cell phone . . .

Sam sighed. No way. Not possible. At least, she hoped not.

She looked back up at Mr. Rothman, who was continuing to display some alarmingly froglike behavior.

Ribbit ribbet, her mystery man added.

LOL. SEND.

The cell phone vibrated again, and Sam choked on her laughter as she read the next message. **I want to hear your laugh. When can we meet?**

Meet? Could she really handle that? She typed in her response, then hesitated for a long moment before pressing SEND. But as the bell rang, she figured, *Why not?*

Soon.

Soon. She couldn't believe it — and she couldn't wait. Sam stood up and brushed herself off, taking one last look around the courtyard, wondering. Was he out there somewhere? Maybe wondering about her?

Then she shook her head, and ran back toward the school. She'd find out soon enough.

♕   ♕   ♕

And in another part of the courtyard . . . another cell phone vibrated, and another text message appeared.

Soon.

He couldn't breathe. He was finally going to meet her. His mystery girl. The girl of his dreams.

He just hoped she wouldn't be disappointed.

chapter six

$\mathcal{T}$he next day, Sam hurried to the library's computer lab as soon as her free period began. As always, she logged in as "Princeton Girl." Would "Nomad" (i.e., Prince Charming) be online?

She breathed a sigh of relief — there he was. She wasn't surprised — sometimes it just seemed like they were totally on the same wavelength. Or maybe he'd just figured that she would be online, since she'd lately been spending *all* her free periods in the library (so okay, she was a little addicted — so what?).

Princeton Girl: You know what really bugs me? The kids who can't get over themselves.

Nomad: Tell me about it. It's like I'll be surrounded by a ton of people and still feel all alone.

Princeton Girl: I'm with you on that one. Hey, Nomad?

Nomad: Yeah, Princeton Girl?

Princeton Girl: Do you think we've ever met?

Nomad: I don't know. Our school has over thirty-five hundred kids.

Princeton Girl: Well, there's a start.

Nomad: I can at least eliminate the guys.

There was a pause, and then:

Nomad: You're not a guy, right? 'Cause if you are, I'll kick your butt.

Sam laughed out loud, drawing suspicious stares from the people around her.

Princeton Girl: I'm not a guy.

♛　　♛　　♛

They'd been forced to end their conversation when the bell rang, but they picked it up again that night. Sam sat entranced in front of the computer, not caring that she was living in the attic or that she had a million hours' worth of homework stacked up around her. Talking to Nomad made her forget all about that.

And in another room across town, "Nomad" sat in front of his computer, equally entranced and equally eager to run away from the realities of his own life.

Princeton Girl: Have you told your dad about Princeton yet?

"Nomad" looked up from his computer to the USC football banners that covered his walls. He shook his head ruefully. The "Princeton" discussion was *not* going to go well.

Nomad: No, he's not an easy person to go up against.

Princeton Girl: Well, my father always encouraged me to speak my mind.

Nomad: I don't think it would work. You see, he's living his life again through me.

Princeton Girl: Talk to him.

Nomad: It's hard. Everyone thinks we're really tight, but I've never been able to connect with him. I don't think he understands me . . . I can't believe I just told you that. I've never told anyone that.

Princeton Girl: It's okay. You can trust me. What time is it?

Nomad: It's about two.

Princeton Girl: Two? We've been instant-messaging each other for five hours!

Nomad: I think we broke our record.

Princeton Girl: I should turn in.

Nomad: I hear you. Sweet dreams, Princeton Girl.

Princeton Girl: Sweet dreams, Nomad.

But he wasn't ready to go offline — it was always so hard to say good night to her. He wasn't surprised they had talked for five hours; he could talk to her all night long and not even notice the time passing. Unlike . . .

His girlfriend. He looked at a picture of the two of them pinned to his bulletin board — she'd stuck it up there for him, telling him it should be the last thing he looked at before he went to bed each night.

She liked to do that. Tell him what to do.

Everyone in his life did.

Everyone except for "Princeton Girl."

He looked at the picture again, then noticed the flyer hanging next to it, an announcement of the upcoming Halloween dance. And suddenly, he knew what he wanted to do. What he had to do.

He took down the photo and threw it in a desk drawer, then turned back to his keyboard, typing feverishly.

Now the ball was in her court.

♕   ♕   ♕

Sam finished brushing her teeth and headed back to her "bedroom," yawning. She couldn't believe that it had gotten so late — the long and wonderful conversation had passed in a heartbeat.

She was about to climb into bed when she noticed an instant message blinking on her computer. More from "Nomad"?

Curious, she returned to her desk and opened the message.

Nomad: Princeton Girl, the time has come

for us to meet. Place: under the disco ball at the Halloween Homecoming Dance. Time: 11 pm sharp.

Oh. My. God.

Sam didn't know what to do. Heart pounding, she backed away from the computer, never taking her eyes off the screen. They were actually going to meet — if she had the nerve. And did she? Let's be honest, she didn't even have the nerve to write him back. Not yet, at least. Instead, she climbed back into bed and turned out the light.

But she knew that tonight she wouldn't be getting any sleep.

👑 👑 👑

WHACK!

Sam sent another ball flying. She'd hoped that some batting practice might help calm her nerves. She was wrong.

"This is great, Sam," Carter called to her for the hundredth time, from his post by the pitching machine. Carter, dressed today like a hippy, stuck out on the softball field like a sore thumb — but he hadn't complained (well, okay, he had complained, a lot, but only for the first hour or so) when she dragged him down here, and he was doing his best to cheer her up and calm her down. "You're finally going to meet him."

WHACK!

Oops. Carter ducked out of the way as the ball whizzed by his left ear, a little too close for comfort.

"I don't know," Sam said. "This guy is too good to be true."

"Look, it's been a month since you guys met in the Princeton chat room," Carter pointed out. "You guys talk all the time. You *know* him."

"But he doesn't know *me*," Sam said. "I mean, what if I meet him and I'm not what he expects? Maybe it's better to keep this whole relationship in cyberspace."

WHACK! Another run batted in. If there'd been a runner. Or a game.

"No! You *have* to go to that dance. This Nomad guy isn't going to stay in one place for long." Carter paused, looking thoughtful. "Look, if it helps, I'll be your escort."

"Really?" Sam asked, suddenly feeling a little more hopeful.

"Really."

Sam smiled in relief. "You rock, Carter."

And that's when her cell phone rang — just when things were starting to look up. She answered the phone and . . .

"WHERE'S MY SALMON!!!!" Fiona's voice came screeching through the phone, puncturing Sam's newfound calm *and* her eardrum.

Fiona hung up immediately, and Sam snapped the phone shut.

"I have to go," she said, resigned.

Carter didn't have to ask why — everyone within a fifty-yard radius had heard Fiona's primal scream — but he also didn't have to like it.

"Sam, why do you act like her slave?" he asked.

"Simple. No Fiona, no money for Princeton."

"That's lame," he said.

Sam smiled ruefully. "Tell me about it."

One last ball shot out of the machine and Sam swung with more force than she'd managed all afternoon.

WHACK!

It soared over a fence and disappeared . . .

♛   ♛   ♛

. . . and landed on the football field, rolling directly toward the captain of the football team himself, Austin Ames, who was getting in some extra practice with Ryan. Could Austin have some stress to burn off, too? Did handsome, popular football team captains even *get* stressed?

"Whoa, a girl hit that?" Austin asked, sweeping up the ball. "Impressive."

"So, what are you and Shelby going to the dance as?" asked Ryan.

Austin hesitated — but there was no time like the present. "I don't think I'm going with Shelby," he admitted.

"Say what? You're not going with Shelby? Who else would you go with?"

Austin threw the ball back to the baseball diamond. "It's a mystery to me."

"Thank you!" a girl's voice called from the softball field.

"You're welcome!" Austin shouted back.

Then he went back to worrying. Who would his mystery date turn out to be?

chapter seven

$\mathcal{I}$t was a big day. The day of the Halloween Homecoming Dance. Which meant big changes were in store — for everyone.

Austin spent the afternoon the way he spent every Saturday afternoon, working at his dad's car wash. Big Andy's Car Wash was the largest car-wash chain in Southern California. It was also the only chain to offer a thirty percent discount for USC football fans (and on occasion, to refuse to serve anyone who made the mistake of supporting the UCLA Bruins, archrivals of USC).

Let's just say that Big Andy liked football — specifically, USC football — a lot.

Austin was taking a break, tossing around the football with one of the other car-wash employees, when his dad walked out and interrupted them, looking none too pleased.

"What's up?" Austin asked.

His father tossed an envelope toward him. It was from Princeton.

"Something you want to tell me?" Austin's dad asked.

Austin squirmed under his father's stern gaze. "I'm just trying to keep my options open."

"You don't need options. Austin, I'm a major contributing alumnus. It's all been taken care of."

When Austin didn't express his undying gratitude — or, in fact, say anything at all — his father continued. "Look, we've been working on this program since you were nine. You're gonna play ball for USC, graduate, then co-manage the family business with me. Your future is set. Don't mess with the plan."

Austin sighed. "Wouldn't think of it."

"Now, go help out with the customers and let's put an end to this nonsense." Big Andy turned away and headed back into his office — there was a game on, after all, and it was just begging him to watch.

"Whatever you say, Dad," Austin muttered, hating himself for not having the nerve to talk back to his father. But, instead of following him inside, Austin did as he was told, and headed toward the entrance to wait on the next customer.

♔   ♔   ♔

Sam pulled into the car wash, relieved to take a brief break from the hideous LA traffic. She'd been driving around town all day, buying Fiona's groceries, picking up Fiona's dry cleaning, and generally driving herself crazy to serve Fiona's every tiniest whim.

As she pulled her car up to the entrance, she saw Austin Ames himself come jogging toward her. Great. Just what she needed to top off an already miserable day — an encounter with the enemy. If she'd known that one of the school's "best and brightest" worked here, she most definitely would have gone somewhere else.

"You could use a wax," Austin said, once he'd had a chance to check out the beat-up old car.

"Uh . . . fine," Sam told him, just wanting to get this encounter over with as quickly as possible. But before he could get started on her car, a horn beeped behind them. They looked over to see two brightly colored VW convertibles — both completely covered in mud.

Sam would have recognized them anywhere — the stepsister-mobiles. And sure enough, there were Gabriella and Brianna, each standing proudly beside a spattered car.

"Austin! Hi!" they called, waving excitedly. "We need our cars washed! Look! Dirt!"

Austin told them they'd have to wait, and got to work on Sam's car. She knew she should just wait there with him, steering clear of the wonder twins, but she couldn't stand the idea of making awkward small talk with someone who clearly didn't understand why people like her even existed.

So, choosing the best of two terrible options, she headed over to talk to Brianna and Gabriella. "What happened to your cars?" Sam asked. "How'd they get so dirty?"

"What are you, the dirt police?" Gabriella said, tittering.

"Yeah," Brianna chimed in, "the dirt police, like . . ." She wracked her tiny brain for an appropriate insult. "Like, excuse me, young lady, do you know how fast your dirt was going?"

There was an awkward silence, as not even Gabriella could bring herself to laugh. "You should have stopped at dirt police," she sneered.

Brianna ignored her. She had something better for Sam, anyway. "You better get going," she told Sam. "Our mom's looking for you, and she is m-a-d *mad*."

Sam wasn't surprised. When was Fiona ever *not* mad?

"Where is she?" Sam asked.

"She's home," Brianna said. "Baking."

Sam retrieved her freshly waxed car, almost eager to get home and find out what that was all about. Fiona, baking? This she had to see.

♛   ♛   ♛

When Sam got home, she found a bikini-clad Fiona in the backyard, lying facedown in a tanning bed. *Baking* under the fake sun. Of course.

"You wanted to see me?" Sam prompted, hoping she was interrupting Fiona's oh-so-precious relaxation time.

"Yes," Fiona replied, not bothering to look up. "Have you finished your errands?"

"Yes, ma'am."

"Stop calling me ma'am," she snapped. "You just do that to make me feel old."

"Sorry." Fiona was being ridiculous . . . but on the

other hand, Sam *did* do that just to make her feel old. Good to know it was working.

"You put the day's receipts in the safe?" Fiona asked.

"Check."

"Picked up my dry cleaning?"

"Check."

"Ordered more salmon?"

Sam suppressed a smile. "Check."

"Good. Now I'll need you to head back to the diner and take the night shift."

Sam couldn't believe it — after all she'd done today? Wasn't that enough? Wasn't anything ever enough?

"Tonight's the night of the Halloween Homecoming Dance," she protested.

"Sam, please try to not be so inconsiderate," Fiona interrupted. "Tonight's a busy night for us. We need the manpower."

"But I really need to go to this dance!" Sam pleaded.

"But I really need to go to this dance!" Fiona repeated, mockingly. Then her voice got serious — and cold. "What you *need* is tuition money for college. This isn't a gravy train I'm running."

Sam couldn't take it anymore. "Fiona, I'm a straight-A student, I work seven days a week, I'm taking extra AP classes so I can graduate early, and I never ask for anything." She took a deep breath. "Why won't you ever let me do anything fun?"

Fiona wasn't even fazed. "Sam," she began, in a sugary sweet voice dripping with venom, "you're not very pretty and not very bright. I know it hurts. But I'm just trying to protect you."

"But . . ." Sam's voice trailed off. What could she say to that?

Nothing, apparently. "This discussion is over," Fiona said with finality.

Dejected, deflated, defeated, Sam slipped away.

Fiona hit the remote that would lift up the top of the tanning bed so she could turn over. The machine whirred furiously, but nothing happened.

"Oh, come on," Fiona growled. She hit the remote again. And again. Still nothing. Finally, she gave up, forcing the top open with her hands until the mechanism kicked in.

"And get this bed fixed!" she called out as Sam disappeared into the house.

Her evil work done for the day, Fiona sighed in contentment and rolled over onto her back. She hit the remote again and this time, the bed indeed responded — all too soon. The top of the bed slammed down on top of her, hitting her in the face.

"My nose!" she shrieked.

It was classic — and it would have made Sam the happiest girl in the world for at least an hour . . . if she had only seen it happen.

♕ ♕ ♕

So that evening, Sam found herself trapped at the diner, rolling through the kitchen with an armful of dirty dishes rather than getting ready for the night that could change her entire life. Figures. Just when it seemed like something good was about to happen, Fiona stepped in and ruined it.

Lost in thought — well, more accurately, lost in bitterness — Sam almost crashed into the wicked step-mother herself, who'd deigned to come down and spend an hour or two supervising the staff.

"Would you please watch where you're going?" Fiona snapped, jumping backward.

"Sorry, Fiona." Sam noticed that her stepmother was wearing a Band-Aid over her nose, which had turned a nasty shade of black and blue. It looked painful — a fact from which Sam tried not to take *too* much pleasure. . . .

"Now, I'll be picking Brianna and Gabriella up from the Halloween Dance. I'll be back by twelve to check on you." Fiona squinted suspiciously at her stepdaughter. "You *better* be here."

Sam nodded, and Fiona whirled around, almost col-liding with Rhonda, who had crept up behind her.

"You've got a booger in your nose," the waitress in-formed her, with a playful glint in her eye.

Fiona cautiously touched her nose, then yelped in

pain, as even the slightest touch to her bruises sent shock waves ricocheting through her body. Rhonda just smiled.

"Where are your skates?" Fiona asked, trying to regain the upper hand.

"If I wanted my butt on wheels, I'd get in my car and drive," Rhonda said.

"It's part of the uniform," responded Fiona, who sensed she was, for once, fighting a losing battle.

"If I wanted a uniform, I would've joined the Army." And without another word, Rhonda walked away, leaving Fiona standing there with her mouth open. She froze for a moment, then stalked out of the diner, slamming the door behind her. Sam swore she could feel the temperature in the room rise a few degrees once the ice queen had departed.

"Girl, how do you put up with it?" Rhonda asked once the coast was clear.

"Why do you think I'm graduating a year early?" Sam said. "So I can get out of here. So I can be three thousand miles away at Princeton."

Rhonda shook her head. "Well, save a seat for me." She turned back to her customers, and Sam knew she should probably do the same. Then she noticed who her next customer was — Austin Ames. Just her luck.

Sam groaned but sucked it up and started heading over to his table — then froze as Shelby, Madison, and Caitlyn glided into the diner. No way was she dealing with them right now, not in the kind of mood she was in. Rhonda could handle it. Eleanor could handle it. Someone else would just have to handle it.

And that's when Eleanor swept past, her arms filled with plates, and nodded over toward Shelby and Austin's table.

"Sammy, dear, I'm desperate! Could you cover that table for me?" Eleanor asked quickly, still moving.

"But . . ."

But it was too late, Eleanor was already gone. Sam looked over at Austin and Shelby's table, her heart sinking. *Well, this is my life*, she thought. *Better suck it up and deal.*

♛   ♛   ♛

"Why do I have the feeling I won't be able to get a Zone meal here?" Shelby complained, cuddling up against Austin while trying not to let any part of her exposed skin touch the table or the seat of the booth. She just knew this place was crawling with germs.

"I already ate," Madison said, throwing down the menu.

"Laxatives don't qualify as a food group, Madison," Caitlyn sniped.

Austin looked totally trapped. "Who said anything about eating?" he asked. "I just wanted to have some time to spend with Shelby — *alone*."

48

He stopped talking as Sam skated toward their table to take their order.

Shelby looked up in disgust. "Well, if it isn't diner girl."

Sam slapped on her best perky grin. "What can I get you guys?"

Shelby wrinkled her nose. "What can I get here that has no carbs, no sugar, and is fat-free?" she asked.

Sam thought for a second, then answered, "Water . . . or air."

Austin tried not to laugh. He knew he shouldn't laugh. But he just couldn't help it.

Shelby pointedly ignored him. "I'll have a bottled water," she told Sam.

Sam skated away, muttering — but she didn't get very far before Shelby called her back.

"Oh, diner girl!"

Sam returned, looking at Shelby expectantly.

"Some lemon on the side," Shelby requested, smiling sweetly.

Sam nodded and skated away. And then —

"Oh, diner girl!"

Sam turned around again, almost falling over on the sharp curve, but righted herself just in time and returned to the table.

"Yeah?"

"Make sure it's bottled."

Sam looked like she desperately wanted to say something, but instead she just pressed her lips together very tightly, whipped around, and skated away.

Austin jumped in before the conversation could get away from him again — he had to get this taken care of, before he completely lost his nerve.

"Shelby, I need to talk to you — *privately*," he insisted.

Shelby just laughed. "Anything you say to me you can say in front of my girls."

"I really don't think it's a good idea," Austin said doubtfully.

"Austin, relax. Just close your eyes, take a deep breath, and tell me your thoughts."

Austin shook his head. If this was the way she wanted it . . .

"Okay." He closed his eyes and took a deep breath. "I want to break up."

He opened his eyes — he couldn't read Shelby's face. She didn't look upset, just . . . irritated. Seriously irritated.

"Are you in love with somebody else?" she asked.

Austin decided it was best to be honest. "Possibly."

Now Shelby looked ready to pounce. "Who is it?"

"I don't know . . . yet." Austin paused, wondering what to say next. "I hope we can be —"

Shelby grabbed him by the shirt and pulled him toward her, their faces only inches apart.

"If you say the word 'friend,' I'll kill you," she hissed. "Now, fortunately for you, I'm going to overlook this mental breakdown of yours. Consider yourself forewarned. I'll see you at the dance."

She gestured toward Madison and Caitlyn, and the two girls scurried to follow her as she stood up and stalked out of the diner.

♛   ♛   ♛

Sam came out of the kitchen with the bottle of water — lemon on the side — just in time to catch Shelby and the girls leaving the restaurant. Typical. There went ten minutes of her life that she'd never get back.

A moment later, Austin got up and headed toward the door himself. As he reached for the door, it flew open in his face, and Carter — decked out in full Zorro costume, cape, mask, sword, the works — burst into the restaurant.

"Have no fear, Zorro is —"

Zorro was crashing into Austin Ames — the type of collision that tends to destroy a dramatic entrance.

Austin edged around him, disappearing out the door before anything else could stop him. Carter barely noticed.

"I'm going to try that again," he said, stepping back outside the restaurant and then bursting back in.

"Have no fear, Zorro is here! And he's got keys to his dad's Mercedes." That's when Carter caught sight of Sam, still wearing her oh-so-classy poodle skirt and roller skates. "You're not going to the dance dressed as a wait- ress, are you?" he asked.

"I'm not going," Sam said in a deflated monotone.

"What do you mean you're not going? What about your Cyberdude?"

Rhonda overheard him and veered toward them — there was no way she was missing out on the gossip.

"What's a Cyberdude?" she asked.

Carter grinned, eager to have someone else on his team. "Her secret admirer. He wants to meet her . . ."

"And . . ." Rhonda prompted.

"And I have to work," Sam pointed out.

"But this is your true love," Carter argued.

"Well then, true love will have to wait."

Rhonda slammed her fist down on a table. "That does it! A person can only take so much." She turned toward Sam. "You are *going* to that dance. I am sick to death of that woman taking advantage of your good nature."

"You tell her, girlfriend!" Carter cheered.

Rhonda shot him a dirty look.

"Guys, I can't go," Sam protested. "If Fiona finds out I'm not here, she'll make my life miserable."

"Like it's not right now?" Rhonda asked.

"You tell her, girlfriend!" Carter cheered again.

Rhonda — not a small woman by any means — took a threatening step toward him. "You call me 'girlfriend' one more time and . . ." Her voice trailed off, but as she towered over Carter, she got her point across.

Then Rhonda softened, putting her arm around Sam. "Look, Sam," she said in a low voice. "You were everything to your father. Everything he did, he did for you." Sam nodded, tears in her eyes. "But now he's not here. So the things he would have done, you're going to have to do for yourself. And I *know* that if he were here, you'd be going to that dance."

By this time, the rest of the diner employees, attracted by all the shouting, had crowded around Sam and Rhonda.

"You're always studying or working," Bobby added in. "It's time for you to do something for yourself."

"I never do anything for myself," Sam said slowly, as if just realizing it.

"No, you don't," the group chorused.

"I deserve to go out," she said, a little more boldly.

"Yes, you do," her friends encouraged.

"You know what?" Sam grinned, a little of the old, tough Sam coming back into her eyes. "I'm going to go."

"Yeah!" the group cheered.

Then Sam's face fell. "Not."

"Why not?" everyone asked, in a single voice.

"I don't have a costume."

Dead silence. How could you go to a costume ball and meet the love of your life . . . if you didn't have a costume?

Then, very slowly, a smile crept its way across

Rhonda's face. She turned away from the group, toward the diner's remaining customers.

"EVERYBODY OUT!" she boomed. "Time to go! Don't worry about the bill, it's on the house — just get up and go. Right now."

No one moved. Who'd ever heard of kicking all the customers out of a restaurant? They were confused, they were mystified, they weren't sure what to do, but they were still seated. Until —

"WE'VE GOT A RAT!" Rhonda shouted.

And chaos ensued.

Moments later, the restaurant was deserted, except for Sam, Carter, the staff, and one large, large man eating his pie in the corner, reading a paper. Rhonda rolled her eyes and went up to the table, grabbing his plate of pie.

"I'm not finished," the guy complained.

"Oh, yes you are!"

♛   ♛   ♛

Rhonda, Sam, and Carter arrived at the costume shop just as the clerk was locking up. Not that that stopped Rhonda.

"Vernon, Sam needs a costume," she said.

Vernon was a tired-looking older man who looked like he just wanted to go home and go to bed.

"Rhonda, it's Halloween night," he complained wearily. "There's nothing — and I'm closed."

"Free breakfast for a week?" Rhonda wheedled.

Vernon barely hesitated for a moment before unlocking the door. "Make that a month."

The three friends barreled into the store, then stopped cold in the doorway as they surveyed the rows and rows of empty racks. Vernon wasn't kidding — this was going to be a challenge.

Still, there were a few costumes left . . . and Sam tried them all on for size.

Freddy Kreuger.

"I wanted to be the girl of his dreams, not his nightmares," Sam pointed out.

Matador.

"It's a dance," Sam said. "Not a bullfight."

Rhinoceros.

Cockroach.

Turtle.

"At least you're coming out of your shell," Carter joked.

Skintight leather-clad video game action heroine.

This one was the last straw.

"I . . . can't . . . breathe . . ." Sam gasped, dropping to the floor melodramatically.

Soon they'd run through all the costumes, and had found nothing.

"Rhonda, this is hopeless," Sam said. She was ready to give up and go back to the diner. But Rhonda was no quitter — and she'd just had her best idea of the night.

The racks may have been empty, but the wall was still covered with dozens of colorful, glittering masks — and Rhonda grabbed the glitziest, most glamorous mask of all.

"I don't have the rest of that costume," Vernon warned.

"Well, I do!" Rhonda said, grinning. "Let's go!" She handed the mask back to Vernon, grabbed Sam's hand, and led her out of the store.

The three of them drove to Rhonda's house and, leaving Carter to wait in the car, Rhonda and Sam went inside to dress Sam for the ball.

As Rhonda rummaged around in the bedroom, Sam waited in the living room, admiring the way Rhonda had filled her living room with beautiful paintings and knick-knacks. The room itself was like a work of art.

"You sure have a knack for taking something plain and making it beautiful," Sam called out to her.

"Thanks!" Rhonda emerged from the bedroom carrying a large box. "This was my mother's wedding dress. She always wanted me to put it to good use."

Sam was taken aback — she hadn't expected anything like this. "Rhonda, I couldn't."

"Please, Sam. You'd be doing me an honor."

Sam didn't know what to say. She gave Rhonda a hug, holding her tightly for several moments before letting go.

"Talk about my fairy godmother," she said finally, her voice choked with emotion.

Rhonda looked a little embarrassed and began searching through a pile of boxes. "All we need is one final touch." Soon she'd found the box she was looking for, and opened it with a dramatic flourish. "Ah, the pièce de résistance!"

She lifted out a beautiful, jeweled mask. It glistened in the light as if it was covered with diamonds.

Sam took it from Rhonda with trembling hands. She had everything she needed for her costume . . . now it was time to go meet Prince Charming.

chapter eight

$\mathcal{J}$t was called the Valley Royale Hotel, but it looked like a castle.

And deep inside, hundreds of costumed students whirled the night away in a fabulous, star-spangled ball-room.

It was bound to be a magical night.

"Welcome, North Valley High School seniors, to the annual Halloween Dance!" There was Astrid, spinning records up onstage and trying to rally the students . . . in her own special Astrid way. "Tonight a panel of our esteemed teachers will use their years of higher education to pick out a Prince and Princess of the dance, thus making the rest of us feel terrible about our already meaningless lives."

A spotlight hit the row of teachers standing by the stage as a few weak bursts of applause trickled through the room.

"In true LA fashion," Astrid continued, "it's not only about what you wear, but who you are."

And with that, she turned up the music again — and the crowd went wild.

♛ ♛ ♛

Shelby, Madison, and Caitlyn had struggled a long time with their costume choice. But finally they'd decided — or, rather, Shelby had decided for them.

"Charlie's Angels, right?" said some kid dressed as Einstein.

"What are you, some kind of genius?" Shelby asked sardonically. She pulled out a compact and checked herself out in the mirror.

"How do I look?" she asked the girls.

"Dressed to kill!" they chorused.

Shelby nodded. Time to get down to business. "Where is he?"

And, Madison and Caitlyn following a suitable distance behind, she took off through the crowd in search of her prey.

♛ ♛ ♛

"Okay, how are we supposed to do this, genius?" Brianna asked her sister, pointing toward the stars. Brianna and Gabriella were dressed as cats. More accurately, they were dressed as *one* cat, with two heads. From the head up, they looked pretty cute, with their spunky cat ears and frisky whiskers. But from the head down? That was another story. Squeezing into a single costume proved more difficult than they'd expected. Each leg of the cat had two of their legs in it, which meant that instead of walking, they had to hop. Making it pretty difficult to get anywhere. Like down the stairs.

Brianna looked dubiously down the staircase, then hopped down the first step. "Like this."

"I can't believe I let you be in charge of the costumes," Gabriella complained. "I'm such an idiot."

"I remember it very clearly," Brianna said defensively. "I said, 'How about a Siamese cat' and you said okay."

"Right, Siamese *cats*, not Siamese *twins*."

Gabriella paused for a second, looking confused. "Hey, are we having a catfight?"

♛ ♛ ♛

Austin, Ryan, and David had planned to be the Three Musketeers. Emphasis on *had*. Austin, unfortunately, was decked out in tight pants, a frilly shirt, and a cape. What was he supposed to be? Who knows. But definitely *not* a musketeer.

"Sorry about your costume getting lost, Austin," Ryan said.

"It's not a big deal," Austin told him, distracted. He had better things to think about than a stupid costume. Things like *her*. Where was she? Who was she?

"This sucks," David said. "Now we're the two musketeers and their wimpy friend who wears tights."

But Austin barely heard him. He was too busy looking around the ballroom, wondering.

And waiting.

♛   ♛   ♛

Sam hid under Carter's cape for the whole ride to the hotel, but once they arrived, it was time to unveil herself.

Except that she didn't want to.

"Sam, will you take my cape off already?" Carter urged. "You look amazing."

Sam gave him a strange look. "Carter, *you're* not Nomad, are you?"

Carter laughed. "Sam, we've been friends since we were eight. You're like my sister."

Sam smiled. Carter was right, it was a crazy idea. "Sorry, I'm just freaking out a little bit. Don't forget, I need to be back at the diner by twelve."

"Give me your cell phone," he suggested.

She hiked up her dress (it's hard not to be ladylike when you're wearing a wedding dress, but Sam seemed to manage) and pulled the phone out of her garter belt.

"I'll set the alarm on it," Carter explained. "Quarter to twelve. Now, give me the cape back. . . . It's time."

♛   ♛   ♛

Brianna and Gabriella had made it down the stairs intact — well, pretty much intact — and were on a mission.

They hopped past Mrs. Wells, one of the costume contest judges, and oh-so-subtly dropped a twenty-dollar bill at her feet.

"Girls," Mrs. Wells called out after them, "you dropped this." She waved the bill at them.

"Are you sure?" Gabriella asked, winking hard in Mrs. Wells' direction. "I think that's *your* twenty-dollar bill . . . if you catch my drift."

Mrs. Wells shrugged her shoulders and pocketed the money. "Thank you."

Brianna leaned toward her sister. "I don't think she caught the drift," she whispered.

But before they could take their bribery to the next level, Mrs. Wells was distracted by a commotion by the entrance. "Who is that charming young lady?" she asked, pointing at the figure descending the stairway.

The dancing abruptly stopped as everyone's attention was captured by the new arrival. They gazed up at the stairs, overcome by a beautiful vision in white lace. She wore a long dress that made her look like a princess and a jeweled mask that scattered the light into a glowing aura around her gleaming golden hair.

Who was she?

She was, of course, Sam. And she was spectacular.

Midway down the stairs, Sam suddenly noticed that she was the center of attention.

"Carter, what's everybody staring at?" she asked from behind her mask.

"You."

And he was right. The room was in awe.

Gabriella and Brianna couldn't take their eyes off of her.

"I know that girl from somewhere," Gabriella said.

"I've seen her before," Brianna agreed.

Even Shelby and her friends were captivated.

"I love her dress," Madison gushed.

"Who is she?" Caitlyn wondered.

"I think she's from Beverly Hills," Shelby said knowingly.

Madison and Caitlyn looked at each other, stars in their eyes. "90210 . . ." they gasped. This girl really *was* a princess!

♕   ♕   ♕

Carter led Sam through the crowd to the center of the dance floor. Right under the disco ball, where she had a date with Mr. Wonderful.

"You sure I look okay?" she asked Carter one last time.

He looked her up and down, admiringly. "Sam, he'd be a fool not to fall for you." He gave her a hug, and then disappeared off into the crowd.

Sam was left alone under the disco ball. Wondering. And waiting.

And then — a voice behind her. A guy.

"Did you know you're standing directly below the disco ball?"

She smiled and turned around, ready to meet her future.

And there was Terry the techno-stalker, dressed like Keanu Reeves in *The Matrix*. Only not hot.

Sam couldn't believe it. Could *not* believe it. Terry?

"It seems that fate has brought us together, right here, at this anointed hour, under the shimmering disco ball," Terry said, gazing into her eyes.

Trying not to be overwhelmed by a flood of horror and disappointment, Sam forced a smile. "Are you really . . . Nomad?"

"Nomad?" Terry repeated. "Why, I haven't been called that since they canceled *Deep Space Nine*. Now join me in the mating dance of Zion." He held out his arms to her. "Galaxies have been lost and won because of this dance."

Terry grabbed Sam and started to do . . . could it be? The techno-geek version of the Lambada? Could her life get any more ludicrously pathetic?

Sam extricated herself from Terry's tentacles. "Could you get me something to drink?" she asked.

"Some libations for the fair maiden? Your wish is my

command." And he scurried off into the crowd, hopefully never to be seen again.

"I knew this was too good to be true," Sam muttered to herself.

And that's when she heard it. Heard him.

"Princeton Girl?"

A voice behind her. Sam turned around — telling herself that no one, *no one* could be worse than Terry.

Wrong.

"Austin Ames?" she asked incredulously. "*You're* Nomad?"

Austin's face fell. "Don't sound so thrilled."

Sam began to back away. "I'm sorry, but I think this was a mistake. I've got to go."

"Wait!" Austin said desperately, reaching out for her. "It's not a mistake."

"Don't you know who I am?" Sam asked.

But of course, he didn't — her face was hidden behind the glittering mask. And as far as she was concerned, it was going to stay that way.

"Of course I know who you are," Austin lied confidently. "You're . . . you're the girl whose dad owns that mansion in Malibu? The one who throws the cool parties?"

"No."

If at first you don't succeed . . .

"Wait a minute, I got it!" Austin said triumphantly.

"Ferrari girl! You're Fer —" Catching her scornful look, he stopped. "I guess not."

"You have no idea, do you?" Sam said.

Austin met her gaze defiantly. "Yes, I do. You're Princeton Girl. You're the girl I've been waiting to meet. What's your name?"

Before she was forced to answer, Terry returned with her punch. Saved by the geek.

"Your sweet libations, m'lady," he said, offering her a cup. Then Terry noticed Austin. Noticed Austin gazing at Sam and Sam gazing at Austin.

"Austin Ames with m'lady," he said in a robotic voice. "Mission abort."

Terry bowed deeply, then left them alone. Together.

"What about your girlfriend?" Sam asked, deftly avoiding the name question for the moment.

"My girlfriend?" Austin asked. He'd forgotten all about her. Forgotten everything that wasn't the beautiful girl in front of him.

"Shelby," Sam prompted.

"It's over," Austin said distractedly. He was entranced. He was enchanted. He was in love.

Of course, it wasn't over. It would never be over until *Shelby* decided it was over. And that time had definitely not come.

But neither Austin nor Sam realized that Shelby was in the balcony watching them through binoculars. She hadn't taken her eyes off them since they'd met. But they only had eyes for each other.

"I guess you were expecting some guy who hangs out at Starbucks and writes sonnets?" Austin asked his mystery girl.

"Something like that," Sam admitted. "I mean, you're Austin Ames. Football captain. Student body president — and closet poet?" She shook her head. "You can't be both guys."

"I know that," Austin said.

"Well then, who are you?" she asked.

Austin sighed. "I don't know."

That wasn't the answer Sam was looking for, and it certainly wasn't the one she needed. She tried to turn away, but Austin stopped her.

"What I do know," he said, talking quickly and earnestly, "is that through our e-mails we have real conversation. On October 11th I wrote, 'When I talk to you . . . '"

"'. . . I feel I can be myself,'" Sam finished for him. She knew those words by heart.

"Just give me a chance," Austin pleaded.

Sam's head was spinning. How could it be — Austin Ames? Nomad? It just didn't make any sense. And yet, the things he said . . . she *knew* him. And he knew her, like no one ever had. And the way he was looking at her . . .

"I still don't know your name," Austin reminded her.

"I'm Sa —" But Sam couldn't bring herself to say it. "Cinderella."

Austin smiled. "Okay, Cinderella. How 'bout joining me for a stroll outside?"

Sam caught her breath. She'd been hoping he would say that — and dreading it. "But if you want to be voted Homecoming Prince, you should probably stay inside and be seen," she pointed out, stalling for time.

"I don't care about being Homecoming Prince. Let's go." He held out his hand and, after a moment, she took it.

Austin led her outside, into the lush grounds surrounding the hotel. The green grass stretched on forever and a stream sparkling in the moonlight trickled from pond to pond. Weeping willows whispered in the breeze and the lights strung through their branches twinkled like stars.

It was too good to be true.

Except it was.

Austin clasped Sam's hand. "From your e-mails, I feel like I know you so well," he said. "But are you ever going to tell me who you actually are?"

Sam smiled cryptically. "I haven't decided yet."

"Would you tell me if I guessed right?" Austin asked.

"Maybe . . ."

"How about we play twenty questions," Austin suggested.

"How about ten?"

Austin smiled. "I'll take what I can get. Okay, first question." He thought for a moment. "You do actually go to North Valley High School, right?"

"Of course," Sam assured him.

"Just checking. You never know with the Internet. Okay, next question. Were you disappointed when you found out I was Nomad? Be honest."

Sam had to think about it for a second. "Surprisingly, no." And it was the truth.

"Did you vote for me for student body president?"

"Surprisingly, yes." Also the truth.

Austin looked intently at her, trying to figure out whose face might be behind the mask. "Do I know you?" he asked.

"You probably think you do."

"You'd think I'd remember those eyes," Austin murmured. He felt like he was drowning in them.

♕   ♕   ♕

Shelby yawned. This party was getting old, fast. And it didn't help to have to put up with dull, dull David, Austin's dull, dull friend. It was bad enough when she'd had to pretend to be into him when Austin was around — nothing worked better than making boys jealous — but now that it was one-on-one, she had no incentive not to blow him off.

"What are you supposed to be?" Shelby asked, feigning interest.

"I'm a Three Musketeer," David said.

"You don't look like a candy bar," Shelby said, confused.

"So, now that you and Austin are toast, why don't we have our own party, Shelby?" David suggested, inching closer to her. "I've got my mom's mini-van tonight . . ."

Shelby recoiled. "Ew! I'm not hanging out in your creepy mom-mobile."

"Come on, Shelby," David said, slinging his arm around her. "Don't be such a tease."

David pulled her in for a kiss, but Shelby squirmed away.

"Back off, David," she said harshly. "I was just trying to make Austin jealous."

The loser lunged toward her again. Shelby tried to push him away, but David was all over her, and there was no getting around him.

That's when her knight in shining armor swooped in to her rescue.

Carter, dressed as Zorro and totally acting the part, pulled David off of Shelby and — with a very un-Carter-like show of strength — sent him flying.

"The lady said stop!" Carter bellowed theatrically. He pulled out his sword and brandished it in David's direction.

Unfortunately, the sword was made out of plastic. David grabbed it out of Carter's hands and snapped it in two.

"I think I just saw your life flash before your eyes," David growled.

"Oh yeah," Carter said defiantly. "Well, did you see the part where I run away?"

David, never too quick on the uptake, didn't get it. "Huh?"

"Run awa-a-a-a-ay!" Carter called over his shoulder as he bolted away.

It took David a moment, but then he took off in pursuit.

Carter raced to the circular bar and scrambled up onto it. David followed close on his heels, and they chased each other around and around until Carter leaped down inside. He turned back to look up at David, who was grinning down at his trapped prey.

"I'm through running," Carter said solemnly.

David laughed and knelt down on the bar, ready to pounce.

But Carter didn't look too worried. "I hate to tell you this, dude, but I starred in *Pirates of Penzance* three summers in a row." Carter grinned. "Say hello to act two, scene one."

Carter flung up the hatch on the bar, slamming it into David's chin. David flew back off the bar, crashing into a table and falling to his knees. And, in a perfect final blow, a giant pumpkin teetered off the table and landed on top of David's head.

Shelby ran up to Carter. "My hero!" she cried, throwing herself into his arms.

Up onstage, totally oblivious, Mrs. Wells cut off the music and grabbed the microphone. It was time for . . . the judging.

"I was right in the middle of a power jam," Astrid protested. "You just totally harshed my mellow."

Mrs. Wells just ignored her. As usual.

"Good evening," she said to the crowd. "I hope everyone has been having a great time tonight. As you all know, it's almost midnight, and that means it's time to announce who we've selected as this year's Halloween Prince and Princess!"

Before she could continue, a roll of dollar bills flew through the air and beaned her in the head.

"Could you girls give it a rest?" Mrs. Well said, staring pointedly down at Brianna and Gabriella.

👑　👑　👑

Sam felt like she'd been walking with Austin forever — but she also felt like the whole night had flown by in a heartbeat. As they wandered the grounds, they suddenly came across a beautiful white gazebo, strewn with hundreds of flowers and candles. Judging from the rows and rows of folding chairs and the mariachi band packing up, it had been some wedding.

As Sam soaked in the romantic surroundings, Austin still couldn't take his eyes off his princess.

"Any chance I can get you to remove that mask of yours?" he asked.

"On the first date?" Sam said playfully. "I don't think so."

Austin sighed. "Fair enough." He grabbed her hand and pulled her to the altar. "If I ask you to dance, does that count as a question?"

"But there's no music," Sam protested.

"Says who?" Austin turned toward the band and said (in Spanish — very impressive), "One more for the road, please. I really like this girl."

The band smiled and picked up their instruments. Soon, a romantic song was floating through the air. Austin pulled Sam close, and they began to sway back and forth, lost in the music.

Spotting a discarded bridesmaid's bouquet over Sam's shoulder, Austin swept up the flowers and handed them to Sam.

"Do you, Princeton Girl, feel like you did the right thing meeting me tonight?" he asked her solemnly.

"I do." She smiled up at him. "And do you, Austin Ames, have any desire to see me again?"

"Let me think about it," he said, and she froze. Quickly, he grinned. "I'm kidding. I do. I do."

He tentatively reached out his hand to lift up her mask. And Sam was actually going to let him, when —

RING!

Her cell phone. Talk about ruining the moment. Sam hiked up her dress and grabbed the phone. "Not now!" she moaned.

"What?" Austin asked, concerned.

"I've got to go," Sam said. It was the last thing in the world she wanted to do.

"Do you have a curfew or something?"

"Something like that. I'm sorry." She squeezed his hand for a moment, and softly grazed his cheek with her fingertips. "Thank you," she whispered. "This was an amazing night." And with that, she took off, racing back toward the hotel.

"Wait!" Austin called after her. "Where are you going?"

"I'm late!" Sam shouted over her shoulder.

"For what?"

"Reality."

♕   ♕   ♕

Back in the ballroom, Mrs. Wells had doled out almost all the costume awards and was ready to pass out the night's top prizes.

"And best sucking-up costume goes to Neal Greenspan, who came as my parking spot!" she announced.

Neal proudly marched up onstage to accept his trophy. He was wearing gray overalls with two white stripes painted down the side, and had a Styrofoam parking bar-

Even after her evil stepmother and stepsisters moved in with her and her dad, Sam Montgomery knew she was the luckiest girl in the world.

But eight years later, Sam's dad had died and she was on her own with her stepfamily, working in her dad's old diner to earn her keep.

Sam still kept her dad's spirit alive. She believed in his motto — "Never let the fear of striking out keep you from playing the game."

And Sam knew she'd always have her best friend, Carter.

Plus, there was her IM buddy, Nomad. Sam knew he was her soulmate — even though she'd never met him.

Until . . . her Prince Charming suggested they meet at their school's Halloween Ball. Much to Sam's surprise, he turned out to be Austin Ames, the most popular guy in school.

Sam was afraid to tell Austin who she really was. But Austin was determined to find out her true identity any way he could.

But when her stepsisters revealed Sam's secret to the whole school, no one wanted anything to do with her — including Austin.

Austin finally realized he couldn't let his princess get away. It's a fairy-tale ending for Sam!

rier slung over his shoulder with RESERVED FOR MRS. WELLS painted on it. The crowd roared.

"And now, the moment you've all been waiting for," Mrs. Wells said. "Your new High School Homecoming Halloween King and Queen are . . ."

Oblivious to the awards ceremony, Sam raced through the room, looking for Carter. She was so intent on her search, in fact, that she didn't hear the final announcement.

". . . Austin Ames and Cinderella!" Mrs. Wells finished.

Gabriella and Brianna threw their arms in the air, crying, "Fix! Rip-off!" But no one could hear them over the thunderous applause.

Austin rushed into the ballroom, looking for his mystery date. But before he could catch up with her, he was swarmed by a throng of cheering admirers who dragged him toward the stage. He was trapped — and Sam was free to escape.

♛   ♛   ♛

It took a while, but Sam finally found Carter in a corner . . . making out with *Shelby*! She couldn't believe it. Of all the strange things that had happened that night, this might just be the strangest. She noticed that Carter was still wearing a mask of his own, and wondered if Shelby even knew who she was kissing.

What a bizarre night.

Shelby rested her head on Carter's shoulder and closed her eyes, which is when Carter noticed Sam, frantically waving and pointing toward where her watch would be — if she had one. Carter gave her a sad, begging look. Didn't she see that he was in heaven?

Sam put her hands on her hips, miming exasperation. And, with a sigh, Carter finally gave in.

"I'm sorry, my dear, but I must bid you *adieu*," he said gallantly to his lady love.

"A what?" Shelby asked.

"I'm outtie." Carter whipped his cape around and took off after Sam, leaving behind a Charlie's Angel who gazed after her departing hero like a lovesick puppy.

Sam and Carter made it to the staircase, but just when Sam thought she was home free, she spotted Austin pushing through the crowd in her direction.

"Wait!" he called.

But there was no time. Sam raced up the stairs and out of the hotel.

Austin charged after her, stopping to pick up the cell phone that she'd dropped without realizing. He burst through the doors into the parking lot — but it was empty. He was too late.

At least she'd left something behind. Proof that he hadn't imagined her.

Austin cradled the cell phone in his hands. It could be the key. He would find her again. He just had to.

♛ ♛ ♛

By this point, Sam had realized that her cell phone was gone, but that was just too bad — there was no time to go back for it. Every second counted.

Once they'd actually reached the car, Sam could relax a little and absorb the excitement of the night.

"I almost kissed Austin Ames!" she said breathlessly, as Carter started the engine.

But he one-upped her on that one. "I *totally* kissed Shelby Cummings!" he crowed. "So, what did Austin say when he found out you were . . . you?"

Sam blushed. "He didn't."

"You didn't tell him?" Carter asked incredulously. "Why not?"

"I don't know. I . . . I panicked."

Carter pulled the car out of the lot, and they both crossed their fingers that they would make it back to the diner in time. It was going to be a close call.

♛ ♛ ♛

Gabriella and Brianna climbed into the backseat of Fiona's car, a little apprehensive about what their mother would have to say about their failure to win — that is, rig — the costume contest.

"Why isn't there a crown on your heads?" Fiona barked.

"Because we didn't win," Gabriella admitted. "Some girl stole it from us."

"I am very upset about this," Fiona said.

"You don't look upset," Brianna observed. And it was true — bizarrely, although her voice had risen to a fever pitch and her hands were clenching the steering wheel, Fiona's face remained completely serene.

"It's the Botox," Fiona explained. "I can't show emotion for six to eight weeks. But trust me," her voice took on an edge, "I am devastated."

The car pulled up to a stop sign and, as the girls looked out the window, they realized they recognized the face looking back.

"Spam!" they shouted in unison, pointing toward their stepsister.

In the Mercedes, Carter pushed Sam's head down below the window. "Step Monster at three o'clock," he hissed through gritted teeth. "Don't move."

Brianna and Gabriella couldn't tattle on their stepsister fast enough.

"Mom!"

"It's Sam!"

"Over there!"

Fiona turned to look at Carter's car — no Sam. Only Carter, humming to himself. He waved innocently.

"Hi, Mrs. Montgomery," he called out from his car. "Ladies."

And with that, he drove away.

Fiona turned to her daughters with a look of disgust.

"She was in the car!" Gabriella whined.

"We saw her!" Brianna added.

"That's ridiculous," Fiona snapped. "Sam's working tonight. She would never disobey me."

But the twins knew what they'd seen. "She was there!" they cried.

♛　　♛　　♛

Back in Carter's car, Sam was busy freaking out.

"Did she see me?" she asked Carter, her heart pounding a mile a minute.

"I don't think so," Carter reassured her. "But those wannabe Olsen twins might have."

Sam caught her breath. "Carter, listen," she said. "I know you want to take good care of the car, but can't you just step on it?"

Carter looked horrified. "Sam, I'm already going 38 in a *35*!"

♛　　♛　　♛

The twins weren't having any better luck. They were flopping around the car like fish on a sunny dock, but Fiona continued to drive toward the diner at an annoyingly moderate speed.

"Mom, hurry!" Gabriella shrieked. "We've got to beat her back."

"Can't you drive any faster?" Brianna pleaded.

"Girls, settle down," Fiona said. "We'll be at the diner soon enough."

"Soon enough isn't soon enough!" Gabriella yelled. Enough was enough. She twisted around in her seat, leaning toward Fiona and forcing her leg onto the gas pedal, shoving it down to the floor.

With a squeal of rubber, the car lurched forward, the acceleration slamming them back against their seats. Out of control, the car hurtled toward the diner, as its passengers — Fiona included — screamed for their very lives.

Would they make it in time?

Would they make it at all?

♕　♕　♕

The Carter-mobile gently rolled to a stop.

At a yellow light.

Which lasted forever.

And then turned red.

Sam was doing her best not to scream. In a calm voice — or, in as calm a voice as she could muster, she pointed out, "You could've totally made that light."

"FYI, yellow means 'caution,'" Carter informed her, "not 'speed up.'"

"Great, I ask for *The Fast and the Furious* and get stuck with *Driving Miss Daisy*."

Then suddenly, a car sped by them — a car filled with screaming, and suspiciously familiar, women.

Carter's mouth dropped open. "Was that . . . ?"

"Uh-huh."

♕ ♕ ♕

"Get your paw off the gas!" Fiona shrieked, frantically trying to maintain control of the car.

"I can't! It's stuck!" Gabriella moaned.

Suddenly, the diner loomed ahead of them. Directly ahead of them.

"We're gonna die!" Brianna cried.

As their screams rose to a fever pitch, Gabriella finally succeeded in wrenching her paw off the gas pedal — and at the last minute, Fiona whipped the steering wheel around, hard, sending the car screeching into the diner parking lot. It spun a 180 and then, finally, skidded to a stop.

Dead silence.

Fiona, Gabriella, and Brianna looked around them, surprised to see that they were all still alive and intact. No one spoke, no one moved.

And then —

"I need to use the litterbox," Brianna whimpered.

♕ ♕ ♕

Fiona flew into the diner, her feline henchmen following close behind.

Rhonda quickly moved into her path — an imposing obstacle, but Fiona was not to be dissuaded.

"Where is Sam?" she asked, in a voice of doom.

Rhonda smiled quizzically. "What do you mean, where is Sam? Where do you think she is?"

"She better be here!" Fiona responded, trying to edge her way around Rhonda.

"Fiona, have you seen our new salt and pepper delivery system?" Rhonda quickly asked. She held up two shakers . . . the same shakers that had been there for fifteen years. "You put salt in this one and the pepper in this one," she pointed out perkily. "It's a revolution!"

Fiona shot her a nasty look and veered to her left — but Eleanor was too quick for her.

"Did I show you the new shine our floors are getting since we switched to Mr. Clean?" she asked.

"Mom, I smell something fishy," Brianna said.

But Fiona was already on to it. She pushed her way around Eleanor, only to be stopped in her tracks by Bobby, on his way out of the kitchen.

"Fiona, I have terrible news," he said with a solemn look. "The salmon passed away."

"That's it!" Fiona exploded. "When I find that girl, I'm going to wring her —"

DING!

At the sound of the bell, they all looked over to the kitchen pass-through, where Sam — complete with chef's hat and cheesy busgirl uniform — had tossed a sandwich on the counter.

"Order's up!" she called, ringing the bell again.

"Sam?" Fiona asked, confused. "What are you doing back there?"

"Working on my culinary skills," Sam said.

Fiona looked helplessly at her stepdaughter, then shook her head and sighed. Without another word, she and the twins turned and traipsed out of the diner.

And Sam breathed a sigh of relief. She waited until they left to pull off her T-shirt and apron, under which she still wore the princess wedding dress.

Now it was all she had left to remember her perfect, perfect night.

♛ ♛ ♛

Out in the diner parking lot, Carter circled the Mercedes, searching for damage. Finding none, he patted its hood with a self-satisfied grin.

"Thank God we made it," he said to himself. "And not a scratch."

He climbed into the car, threw it into gear, and drove toward the parking lot exit — directly toward Fiona's BMW, which came flying out from around the corner.

Carter swerved, just missing it.

And hitting the pole supporting the diner's giant sign.

He jumped out of the car to inspect the damage,

once again finding none. Thank goodness. "Tonight must be my lucky night," he told himself.

And then, a creaking sound.

Carter looked up at the neon "Fiona's" sign.

It slowly stopped rotating . . . and began to teeter. Just a little.

Then a lot.

With a loud crack, it toppled over, crashing down onto the hood of the Mercedes.

The car was totally trashed.

Fiona, who had stopped her own car after her second near-accident of the night, looked on in disbelief.

"Mrs. Montgomery," Carter called out, "your sign hit my car!"

It was the perfect end to a perfect night.

Not.

chapter nine

*M*onday morning — and it was as if nothing had changed. Sam and Carter walked toward the school entrance, fresh from a long battle to find a parking space. Though Halloween had passed, Carter was decked out in costume — this time, it was John Travolta, from *Grease*. Sam hadn't had the energy to force him to change.

Astrid's DJ spiel wafted toward them as they entered the building.

"So, as predicted when he first set foot in the building four years ago, Austin Ames was crowned Prince of the Halloween Dance," Astrid said sarcastically. "But the mystery, though, is who was Austin's Princess? Your loyal subjects, and your Prince, await your ascension to the throne."

Carter turned toward Sam, who had frozen in her tracks. "So, you're not going to talk to Austin?" he asked.

Sam shook her head. "It's not like he's going to be pining for me. Trust me, he's forgotten all about Cinderella by now."

Her resolve lasted about thirty seconds — and then she saw the flyers. The wall was full of them, each with an identical sketch of a girl with a mask. The caption read, HAVE YOU SEEN CINDERELLA?

Carter grinned. "You're right. He's obviously forgotten all about you."

Sam just stared at the wall until Carter finally pulled her away down the hall. They passed the DJ booth, lost in conversation, and thus totally missing the longing look Astrid shot down the hall toward Carter.

"Just remember, people," Astrid said into the microphone, "sometimes the person you're looking for is right in front of you."

♕ ♕ ♕

Austin, David, and Ryan walked slowly down the hall, taping up flyers as they went.

"Why are you going to all this trouble for one chick?" David asked.

Austin bristled. "She's not just some 'chick.' She was . . . real."

Ryan wrinkled his forehead in confusion. "Real, like she still had her old nose?"

"Real," Austin repeated. "Like the kind of girl who has more on her mind than what she wears or how much weight she wants to lose." He paused, as if trying to decide whether it was worth it to continue. "She *listened* to me, you know? I feel like she really understands me."

"Hey, man, I listen to you," David said indignantly. "I feel your pain, I —"

Totally losing his train of thought as a hot cheerleader passed by, David whipped his head around, leering, "Hello, kitty."

"Yeah, you're a great listener," Austin said in disgust.

"Look, man, you found her cell phone," Ryan pointed out. "You gotta get some kind of clue from that."

"The phone is locked," Austin explained. "I just get these text messages like, 'I need you' and 'Come see me now.'"

That caught David's attention again. "Dude, that is so hot."

"That's what I thought," Austin agreed. "Until I got the one that said 'Come fix the fryer.'"

♕   ♕   ♕

As Sam made her way through the hall next to Carter, she couldn't help but feel like everyone was staring at her. Ridiculous as it might seem, she cowered behind one of her books, trying to hide her face from the masses.

Carter just looked exasperated. "He's looking for you everywhere," he said. "You've got to tell him it was you."

"Yeah, right," Sam said. "I'm sure the coolest guy in school is going to be totally thrilled when he finds out his

Cinderella is me. Don't you think it's better to cling to the dream instead of ruining everything with . . . reality?"

Carter put a comforting hand on her shoulder — he knew her life was rough, but enough was enough. "Sam, you can't hide from him forever."

"Like you're one to talk," she retorted. "When are you going to tell Shelby that you're Zorro?"

Carter straightened up proudly. "This morning."

"Yeah, right," Sam said, with a bark of sarcastic laughter. "The day you tell Shelby it was you, I'll tell Austin it was me."

"Deal," Carter said, holding out his hand.

And they shook on it.

👑　👑　👑

Back to Austin, Ryan, and David who were still talking about the mystery girl.

"Look in the yearbook again," David suggested. "Maybe you missed her."

"Maybe she's foreign exchange," Ryan added. "That's hot."

"Totally. It's *le hot*," David agreed.

"No way I missed her," Austin said. "We had a connection."

At that moment, his gaze connected with Sam, who was heading down the hall, right toward him.

Spotting him, Sam panicked and veered off course — walking directly into an open locker.

"Ow!" She swore.

Barely noticing, Austin turned back to David. "Trust me," he said with confidence. "I'd know her if I saw her."

Brianna and Gabriella, having recovered from their own weekend excitement, were down in the school pool, practicing some synchronized swimming.

And, judging from the screaming, splashing, and crashing, they needed the practice.

"After the turn, it's the flying butterfly rollover!" Gabriella complained, disentangling herself from her sister.

Brianna coughed up a lungful of water. "No it's not. It's the mermaid plunge!"

"I can't wait for my solo career," Gabriella said, shooting her sister a murderous look.

And with that tentative truce in place, they took a deep breath and dove back underwater to continue the world's most unsynchronized synchronized swimming routine.

♛   ♛   ♛

Shelby, Madison, and Caitlyn, decked out in the season's hottest designer swimsuits, glided by without even noticing. They had their own problems.

"He was so mysterious," Shelby told her friends. "But really kind of . . . obvious, at the same time. Kind of dangerous. But very safe."

Sam and Carter were watching from the other side of the pool, and Sam looked at her friend in disbelief.

"I can't believe you're really going to tell her who you are," she said, as Carter prepared himself to face the firing squad.

"Sam, once she realizes she's found her Zorro, she'll be thrilled." At Sam's doubtful look, he just smiled. "Watch and learn, my friend."

Carter strolled over to his queen, who was still gushing about her mystery avenger.

"And, wild, but also tame," Shelby continued. "And, oh my God, when I kissed him, I just melted!"

That's when Carter sidled up to them, putting on his cool-as-a-cucumber grin. "What's up, Shelby baby?" he asked.

"Do I know you?" Shelby asked with a sneer.

"Let me refresh your memory." Carter lifted her hand and gallantly leaned down to kiss it.

"Zorro!" he said with a dramatic flourish.

Shelby whisked her hand away. "You mean 'zero!'" she scoffed. "Who are you, anyway?"

"That's Carter Farrell," Madison helpfully pointed out. "He's that guy you cheat off of in Algebra 2."

Shelby looked appalled. "That freak who hums show

tunes? Oh . . . dear . . . God." She whipped around, checking out the room to see how many people had caught her associating with the lord of the geeks. Deciding the coast was clear, she pulled Carter aside for a quick one-on-one.

"Listen, last night I had a very bad cold, I drank a whole bottle of NyQuil, and I just wasn't myself," she muttered quickly. "So anything I did, just pretend it never happened."

"But — we had a connection?" Carter tried to take her hand, but she abruptly pulled away.

"Okay, 'we' don't have anything," Shelby told him. His face crumbled. "'We' are from completely different classes of humanity. Now, let's go back to our usual lives where we only mingle when I copy you in Algebra 2." She gave him a cold smile. "'Kay?"

And with a quick gesture to Madison and Caitlyn, she walked away, leaving Carter standing there on the edge of the pool like an idiot.

Just in time for him to witness the twins' disastrous double flip into the pool . . . which caused a Shamu-sized tidal wave . . . which totally drenched Carter. He slunk back over to Sam, wet and miserable.

"You all right?" she asked with concern.

Carter nodded. "But if she thinks she's still cheating off me, she's crazy!"

♔ ♔ ♔

David and Ryan dragged a reluctant Austin toward a bench in the school's "friendship circle."

The goon squad had hatched their very own plan — which meant that if Austin had any brains at all, he should have been afraid. Very afraid.

"Guys, I don't know about this," Austin said, sitting down on the bench.

"Just trust us," Ryan reassured him.

"We've asked every girl we could find if they were with you at the dance," David explained. "These are the ones who said 'yes.'" He swept his hand toward the field, where a line of girls had amassed. Spotting Austin, they screamed and waved as if they'd just seen Justin Timberlake. As Austin stared in horror, their cries mixed together into a nearly incomprehensible soup of desperation.

"Austin!"

"I love you!"

"I'm Cinderella!"

"Pick me!"

"Pick me!"

"Pick me!"

Austin leaped up from the bench, ready to flee, but Ryan and David pushed him back down. All was going according to their brilliant plan.

David brought out his boom box, and switched on *The Dating Game* theme song.

"Let's bring out Bachelorette number one," he said in his best announcer's voice.

As Austin squirmed under Ryan's death grip, Bachelorette #1 — an unfortunate-looking girl with food-encrusted braces — bounded toward them.

"She's a straight-A freshman who enjoys stamp collecting, quadrangles, and pillow fights," David said. "Please welcome Missy."

Missy clumsily batted her eyelashes at Austin.

"You plus me equals one," she said, in a voice that was probably meant to be sexy, but just came out sounding nasal. Then she lunged toward Austin, sprinkling his face with lipstick-laden kisses until Ryan and David pulled her away.

Austin forced a smile. "Thanks for coming, Missy."

As soon as she was a safe distance away, he shot a vicious glare at Ryan. "You're dead," he whispered.

But there was nothing he could do, because here came Bachelorette #2 . . .

Number two was — as Ryan and David might have put it — a total babe. Hot, blond, and without a single thought in her pretty little head.

"Bachelorette number two enjoys fake people, recess, and sunblock," David said, trying not to drool. "Say hello to Sunshine!"

Sunshine gave Austin a little-girl wave and giggled. "I just go cuckoo for Cocoa Puffs," she told him.

Austin grimaced. "Neat."

Ryan and David couldn't contain themselves any longer. Pushing each other out of the way, they clamored for her attention.

"I'll date you!"

"Marry me!"

"Be my valentine!"

But Sunshine's attention span was a little too short — she'd already forgotten what she was doing there. Ignoring her two idiot admirers, she wandered off the field. The beach was calling. . . .

Just in time, Bachelorette #3 sauntered over. Number three was . . . intimidating. To say the least. Dressed in sweats and a tank top, she looked like she could bench-press more than Austin could — in fact, she looked like she could have bench-pressed *Austin* if she'd wanted to. And she definitely wanted to.

"She's into barbells, World War Two, and protein shakes," David announced. "Heeeeeeeeere's Helga!"

"*Guten tag*, Austin," Helga said, giving him an affectionate slug on the shoulder. The force of it almost knocked him off the bench.

"*Danke schön*," he gasped.

As Helga followed the first two bachelorettes out of sight and out of mind, Austin again glared at his so-called best friends. "You're *so* dead," he muttered.

Oblivious, David continued on to the next name on

his clipboard. "Our next gal's into Cuisinarts, Barry Manilow, and giving detention," he read. "Would you please give a fond hello to"—he paused, looking confused, and more than a little frightened—"Mrs. Wells?"

The three boys turned to stare, horrified, as Mrs. Wells came bounding toward Austin, ready to be his Cinderella.

Austin sighed.

It was going to be a *long* afternoon.

chapter ten

$\mathcal{F}$iona leafed through the mail, stopping as her eyes fell on a letter she'd been waiting for.

It was a thick envelope, and it was marked "Princeton University." Oh, and it was addressed to Sam.

That didn't stop Fiona. Glancing around to make sure no one was watching, Fiona ripped it open, pulling out the cover letter. The first few lines said it all:

"Congratulations, Samantha Montgomery! We are pleased to inform you that you have been accepted to Princeton University. . . ."

At the sound of the door opening, Fiona quickly hid the letter from sight. By the time Sam made it inside, Fiona had regained a casual pose of sorting through the mail.

"Any mail for me?" Sam asked.

"Let's see . . ." Fiona sifted through the envelopes, then looked up at Sam, her eyes wide in shock. "Oh my God!" She paused for dramatic effect. "You've won a million dollars from Publishers Clearing House!"

Sam just rolled her eyes and, pushing past Fiona, headed upstairs to her room.

Once she'd made it to the attic, the first thing she did

was switch on her computer monitor, revealing an instant message from "Nomad." She wasn't surprised — she'd known this was coming. She just didn't know what to say.

NOMAD: I need to know who you are. I can't take my mind off you. Please tell me who you are?

Sam's fingers hovered over the keyboard as she debated what to write. Finally, taking a deep breath, she began, "My name is —"

Before she could type the fateful words, Brianna burst into the room. Sam jumped, immediately closing the IM window. She turned around to see what Brianna wanted. (Brianna, of course, never came into her room unless she wanted something.)

"Sam, are you almost done with my paper?" Brianna whined. "It's due Friday, you know."

"I'm working on it."

"Well, hurry up," Brianna said. "It makes me nervous to have to wait for it."

"Imagine how nervous you'd be if you actually had to *write* it," Sam pointed out snidely.

The comment went completely over Brianna's head. "Oh my God, you're right!" she said in horror.

Sam sighed. "You'll have it in plenty of time."

"This time, try to make it sound a little more like me," Brianna demanded. "I'm tired of explaining why I sound so smart on paper and so not smart . . . not on paper."

"I'll do my not-so-best," Sam assured her.

At that moment, the intercom on Sam's desk — compliments of Fiona — crackled to life.

"Sam, could you come downstairs?"

Guess who.

"Can you give me a minute?" Sam said into the intercom.

"SAAAAAAAAAAM!!!!!!!!" The voice degenerated into a high-pitched squeal, as the inner circuitry of the intercom gave up its battle against Fiona's voice.

Sam reluctantly logged off and stood up from the desk.

"I'll be right back," she promised Brianna.

"Hurry up," Brianna said.

Sam disappeared downstairs, foolishly leaving her stepsister alone in her room. Bored, Brianna sauntered over to the computer screen, where a pop-up asked, LOG OFF. ARE YOU SURE?

Brianna's eyes lit up. Looking over her shoulder to make sure Sam was really gone, she clicked NO, and logged back into Sam's account. Hmm, what to do next?

She clicked on the MAIL icon, and a list of Nomad's messages instantly filled the screen.

"Who the heck is Nomad?" Brianna wondered to herself.

Choosing a message at random, she opened it:

Cinderella, are you not talking to me be-

cause you freaked out when you found out I
am . . . Austin Ames?

Brianna gasped. She was slow — but not that slow.
"Oh my God," she said aloud in disbelief. "Sam is Cinderella!"

She clicked open another e-mail and began to read,
totally absorbed in the electronic soap opera — and totally unaware that, behind the doorway, a devoted twin
was deviously spying on her devious spying.

♛　♛　♛

Brianna pulled up to Andy's Car Wash, eager to meet
the man of her dreams and get started on her new life as a
fairy princess.

"It's me, Austin," she said to herself, practicing. "It's
Cinderella. From the dance. You've found me!"

She got out of the car and headed toward the main
building, continuing her rehearsal.

"You see, Austin, 'I live in a world full of people pretending to be . . . pretending to be . . .'" She drifted off,
looking frantically at the notes she'd scribbled on her
hand. "'Pretending to be something they're not, and I wonder if I have the strength to stop pretending myself.'" She
grinned, as if having just heard the words for the first time.
"Oh, that's good."

She turned the corner, and her smile collapsed.

Austin was leaning against the wall, engaged in a very intense-looking conversation with . . . Gabriella.

How could it be? Her own twin sister, betraying her? Stealing the man of her dreams?

"You see, Austin," Gabriella said, with as much sincerity as she could muster. "I live in a world full of people pretending to be something they're not, and I wonder if I have the strength to stop pretending myself."

Brianna jumped out from behind the corner, pointing an accusing finger at her twin. "You! What are you doing here?"

"What do you mean, what am I doing here?" Gabriella asked innocently. "I'm Cinderella."

"*You're* Cinderella?" Brianna scoffed. "I think that's a hard pill to swallow, considering I'm the most Cinderella-y Cinderella there ever was."

Brianna shoved her sister out of the way.

"Don't listen to this impostor, Austin," she insisted. "*I'm* the real Cinderella."

Gabriella shoved back. Hard. "Don't you remember those e-mails we wrote the other night?" she asked Austin plaintively.

Brianna shoved back *again*, harder this time — but before the wrestling match could begin in earnest, Austin stepped in.

"Okay, ladies, I think I can settle this," he said reasonably. "The girl I met at the dance dropped something on her way out. What was it?"

Gabriella smiled confidently. "Easy. A wallet."

Austin shook his head. "No."

"I mean . . . a wallet-purse," she said.

"Uh, no."

"Oh, um, a fish?" Brianna suggested.

"A fish?" Gabriella asked, full of disdain.

"It was the first thing that popped into my head," Brianna defended herself. "And you said wallet-purse. What is that?" She turned toward Austin, trying to look adorable (and failing miserably). "You see, Austin, she's sick. She needs help. *I'm* Cinderella!"

"*She's* the sicko!" Gabriella protested. "She's just jealous because you picked me!"

The shoving match began again, this time in earnest. The girls were soon so absorbed in their pushing and shoving and complaining and protesting that they failed to notice a relieved Austin slipping away.

"Where'd he go?" Brianna asked when, out of breath, they finally took a break and looked up.

It was a mystery. But, since he was nowhere to be seen, there was nothing to stop them from continuing their war. With a menacing look, Gabriella advanced on Brianna, backing her into the car wash.

"He left," she said accusingly. "You chased him away. Why do you ruin everything?"

Gabriella grabbed Brianna's hand and threw her hard, right into two giant soapy spinning rollers. Brianna was slowly sucked into the soap flaps — and, suddenly, disappeared.

Silence.

"Bri?" Gabriella asked, sounding worried.

Suddenly, a scream. Behind her. Gabriella spun around.

Brianna raced toward her, covered head to toe in soap suds and screaming like a banshee.

Panicked, Gabriella backed away — down the track leading into the car wash. Brianna kept advancing and Gabriella kept backing up, until a blast of red soapy spray shot out from all sides, stopping her in her tracks. Brianna grabbed Gabriella, and they wrestled each other to the ground as the track moved them through the car wash, periodically dousing them with soapy suds.

"Mom should've washed your mouth out with soap a long time ago," Brianna gloated, smashing a handful of soapy bubbles into her sister's face.

Huge brushes began rubbing them back and forth. Oblivious, Brianna and Gabriella continued with their death match.

"I hate you!" Gabriella shrieked.

"I double hate you!" Brianna cried back, in an equally piercing tone.

Suddenly, the bubbles stopped floating. The water stopped spraying. The brushes stopped brushing. All was still and quiet.

Too quiet.

Gabriella turned to Brianna, a look of apprehension on her face. "You didn't happen to order the —"

Brianna nodded.

Both girls' eyes widened in horror. A loud bell rang out above them, and a red light began flashing. It was time for . . .

"HOT WAX!"

Now there was nothing left to do but scream.

♛　♛　♛

Inside the car wash office, Austin looked out the window, wondering if he'd heard something. Something like muffled screaming.

But, seeing nothing, he shook his head and laughed at himself — now he was hearing things? He must be more messed up about this Cinderella situation than he'd thought.

Shrugging, he turned back to the mail, flipping through until he spotted a large envelope — from Princeton.

Holding his breath and closing his eyes, he ripped open the envelope. After a long pause, he forced himself to look down at the letter.

"Yes!" He punched his fist in the air in victory. Accepted! He couldn't believe it.

"Austin!" Big Andy's voice boomed out behind him, and Austin turned around to see his father in the doorway, proudly holding up a sweatshirt.

"Look what I just got at the campus store." He turned the sweatshirt around for Austin to see. It read: USC DAD AND DARN PROUD OF IT.

"What do you think?" he asked his son.

Austin paused. "It's great, Dad."

But he couldn't quite make himself sound like he meant it.

♔ ♔ ♔

Sam couldn't believe it when he walked into the diner. Austin. "Nomad." Whoever he was. The one person she'd been hoping — and dreading — to see.

He sat down in the first empty booth he came to and, sighing, cradled his head in his hands.

Rhonda spotted Sam staring, and looked questioningly at her.

"It's him," Sam mouthed. Rhonda gave Sam a thumbs-up and gestured her over in his direction. She took a deep breath, grabbed a piece of chocolate cake, and decided to go for it.

She approached his table and set down the plate of cake.

"Always cheers me up," she explained.

"Is it that obvious?" Austin asked ruefully.

Sam smiled. "You look like you could use it," she told him. "It's on the house."

Austin shrugged and, grabbing a fork, devoured the cake in four giant bites.

"Feeling better already," he said through a mouthful of cake.

Sam felt like running away, but forced herself to stay. He looked so lost, so alone. "Anything you want to talk about?"

Austin sighed. "I don't know," he said. "I'm just so sick of pretending to be someone I'm not."

He looked up from his cake, catching Sam's eyes for the first time.

"Do you ever just feel like maybe if you take the risk and show someone who you really are, they won't accept you?" he asked.

Sam stared at him. Did she ever feel like that? Was he kidding? How about right at this moment? How about every day of her life?

"Yeah, I do," she admitted.

Austin's eyes swept over her face. "You have something on your cheek," he said softly, reaching up to wipe off a smudge. His fingers grazed her cheek, and lingered. For a long moment, neither of them spoke.

Sam broke the silence. "There's something I should tell you," she began hesitantly.

Austin waited.

After a long pause, she said, "I'm Ci —"

"SAM!!!!!!!!!!!" Fiona's holler ricocheted through the restaurant, jolting Sam out of her confession.

"One second!" she called back to the kitchen.

But it was too late — the moment had passed. When she turned back to Austin, he was laying his money down on the table. "I've gotta book," he told her, getting up to leave. "Thanks for the cake, Sam."

"You're welcome."

What else could she say?

chapter eleven

The next morning, as soon as the bell marked the end of first period, Sam raced out of her class and took off in search of Carter. She spotted him outside his math class, dressed like — a jock? No stranger than usual, Sam supposed. Besides, she had other things on her mind.

"Carter, I talked to him!" she cried. "Not as Cinderella. I talked to him as *me*, Sam. And he didn't hate me."

"So you told him everything?" Carter asked.

"Well . . . no. Not everything. Not the part about me being Cinderella. But I'm going to tell him." A new resolve filled her voice. "After the pep rally. Come with me?"

"Do you even have to ask?"

♛   ♛   ♛

Out in the quad, Gabriella and Brianna were slumped under a tree, sniffling through their very own pity party. As Shelby, Caitlyn, and Madison hovered over them, waiting for them to get to the important part, the twins poured out their story.

"And then she told us that she was going to steal

Austin away from you if it was the last thing she did,"
Gabriella sobbed to Shelby.

"She's always been jealous of you," Brianna added,
wiping away her fake tears and blowing her nose.

Shelby tapped her foot impatiently. "Go on," she
prodded.

"Well, that's when she invented the whole Cinderella
plot," Gabriella explained. "She got ahold of Austin's
e-mail address and started the affair."

"We wanted to tell you earlier, but she threatened to
kill us. She's a *monster*!" Brianna cried.

"If you don't believe us, take a look at this. Her name
is Sam Montgomery." Gabriella grimly handed Shelby a
folder, shielding the handoff with her body as if she was
slipping Shelby a top secret government document.

"Can we be a part of the cool crowd now?" Brianna
asked eagerly. The smile dropped off her face as Gabriella
smacked her in disgust.

But Shelby didn't even notice. She was too busy leaf-
ing through the file of Sam and Austin's e-mails. She looked
disgusted — and angry. Very angry.

"So that little boyfriend-stealer on wheels thinks she
can pull a fast one on me, does she? Well, we'll just see
about that." Shelby's voice was filled with venom. Things
like this didn't happen to girls like her. The person respon-
sible was going to pay.

Soon.

chapter twelve

*S*am had never been to a pep rally before. And now she remembered why.

The drum line's rhythm echoed through the air as the cheerleaders leaped and shouted and the crowd roared in support of the North Valley Fighting Frogs.

"Who we gonna beat?" Coach Berg shouted.

"South Bay!" the crowd thundered back.

"When we gonna beat 'em?"

"Friday!!!!"

The noise was deafening, electrifying — or would have been if you cared about the football team, or had any school spirit, or weren't afraid that you were about to make the biggest mistake of your life.

Unfortunately, Sam didn't fall into any of those categories.

She spotted Austin down in the front row with the rest of the football team. He was turned around in his seat, talking to his father.

Sam, of course, was too far away to hear what Big Andy had to say. But Austin heard every word, loud and clear.

"Good news, Austin," his father shouted over the noise. "I just talked to the head scout. You win the game on Friday, and your future as a USC quarterback is set."

"Great." Austin turned back around to face the field — and his future.

Back up in the stands, Sam felt like she was about to crawl out of her skin.

"You're shaking," Carter pointed out.

"Sorry, I'm just nervous," she said.

"Relax, you're going to be fine." He suddenly jumped up and, at the top of his lungs, shouted "Kill the Lancers!" Then he plopped back down again. "I love this primitive stuff," he told her with an embarrassed grin.

Down on the field, the drums finally stopped drumming and the cheerleaders stopped cheering. Coach Berg stepped up to the microphone to make an announcement.

"Our cheerleaders have prepared a little skit to help us get in the spirit." He ceded the mic to Shelby, who skipped up carrying a large, cardboard storybook. Madison and Caitlyn took their places behind her, holding giant cue cards.

"Once upon a time," Shelby pretended to read from the book, "there was a big, strong, fighting frog. He had a beautiful girlfriend, and his dad owned the biggest pond in all the land. But he still wasn't happy."

Madison and Caitlyn flipped over their first cue card, which read, AWWWW! The crowd obliged.

Brianna bounded onto the makeshift stage dressed as Austin, complete with football jersey, shoulder pads, and football.

Shelby continued. "If only he could find a princess. Then she could kiss him, turn him into a prince, and they could run away together. One night, after the slimy frog ditches his senior poll most popular girlfriend, he meets his princess."

Another cue card: APPLAUSE!

The crowd clapped approvingly.

Now Gabriella appeared on the field, wearing a garish, raggedy Cinderella dress.

"Your Highness," Brianna-as-Austin said solemnly.

Gabriella curtsied, her hoop skirt flying up to expose incredibly cheesy underwear. The crowd burst into laughter.

"Alas," Shelby said. "It turned out that our frog not only had a secret identity but also had a secret e-mail relationship with a pen pal named Princeton Girl . . ."

Sam watched in disbelief. She'd had a bad feeling about this from the start, but it looked like things were about to get much, much worse than even she had thought possible.

Brianna and Gabriella walked to opposite sides of their stage and pretended to type text messages on cell phones.

Brianna-as-Austin called out, "'Dear Princeton Girl, I

can't wait till we finally get to meet. Only you understand the real me. The me who doesn't want to play USC football. The me who really wants to be at Princeton with you.'"

Sam froze. How was this possible? How could they have gotten her e-mails?

She couldn't do anything to stop it — and she couldn't tear her eyes away — it was like watching a car crash in slow motion. Only she was the one crashing.

"'Dear Nomad,'" Gabriella read, aping Sam's voice. "'I want you to know who I am, but I'm scared you'll reject me. You see . . . I've never had a *real* kiss before. To be honest, I've never had a boyfriend.'"

"Awwww!" went the crowd, obeying the next cue card.

Sam and Carter were horrified. "I can't believe they're reading my e-mails," she hissed. "This is so humiliating."

Carter put an arm around her and pulled her close — but there was nothing he could say, nothing he could do. He spotted Austin down in the front row. At least it didn't look like he was taking things any better.

And Shelby wasn't finished, not by far. "That night, our frog tried to kiss the princess, but she ran away."

Gabriella ran away as Brianna called after her, "Princess, princess? Where art thou, princess?"

"But our princess was too scared to come out of hiding, because she had a secret, too," Shelby explained. "She wasn't royalty at all — but a geek, loser, servant girl."

Gabriella rolled back out onto the stage, now dressed

in Rollerblades and a cheesy waitress outfit (cheesier than the real one, if such a thing was possible), carrying a tray with an enormous milk shake.

The crowd applauded on cue.

"And who, may you ask, is this impostor?" Shelby asked. "Well, we've found her. Waiting to claim her home-coming crown, give it up for — the pretend Princess, Diner Girl . . . Sam Montgomery!"

Shelby pointed up into the stands as the crowd ex-ploded in laughter. They began to chant, "Diner girl! Diner girl! Diner girl!"

As the noise rose, Sam felt as if the world was closing in around her. She couldn't move. Couldn't think. Couldn't breathe.

As a single tear slid down her cheek, Carter looked her squarely in the eye. "Ignore them," he said firmly. "You're better than them."

Sam nodded, allowing Carter to take her by the hand and lead her down from the stands. At least she wasn't completely alone in the world. No matter how it felt.

They'd almost made it through the crowd when they noticed Austin rise and step up to the microphone. They froze.

"All right, all right, everybody," Austin said. "Calm down."

The crowd quieted, looking expectantly down at their star quarterback.

"You girls are pretty funny," he said. "But the truth is . . . the truth is . . ."

Austin looked at Coach Berg, who seemed confused and impatient.

He looked at his father, who urged him to get on with it.

And he looked at Sam, who looked — who looked like she was drowning.

"The truth is," Austin finally said, "I don't know what they're talking about." He gave the crowd that cocky Austin Ames smile they loved so much. "I mean, come on, give me a break, do I sound like I'd write that stuff?"

Over the wild applause of the crowd, Austin continued. "This is crazy, 'cause next year, I'm playing ball for USC!"

With that, Coach Berg ran up on the stage, threw his arm around an embarrassed Austin, and yelled into the mic. "Who we gonna beat?"

"South Bay!" the crowd roared.

"When we gonna beat 'em?"

"Friday!!!"

The drum line thundered into action. The cheerleaders threw themselves into a cheer. The crowd went wild. And Austin watched Sam drift toward the edge of the crowd, away from the field — and out of his life.

chapter thirteen

*S*helby met Austin at his locker the next morning, just like in the old days. She was prepared to be generous.

"I want you to know, Austin, there've been mistakes made," she said. "Mostly by you. But the point is, I'm here for you now."

Austin barely heard her. He'd been operating on automatic pilot all morning. Then, as he shut his locker, he saw the one thing with the power to snap him out of his daze: Sam.

He watched her trudge down the hall, shirking from the stares and whispers of the other students, looking exactly the way he felt — totally, completely, abysmally alone.

Shelby followed the direction of his gaze, and sneered.

"People like her don't belong in our world," she reassured him.

"You're right about that, Shelby," Austin said softly. "She's better than us."

It had been the longest day of her life. All day long, their stares had burned into her, the gossip had swept over her — and Sam had done her best to stay invisible. Not too hard, since she'd been doing it most of her life.

Now she'd finally made it home, and all she wanted was to slink up to her room and hide under the covers for the rest of her life — or at least until it was time to face the world again the next morning.

Noticing a pile of mail on the coffee table, she stopped to sift through it, and spotted a letter from Princeton.

Could this be it? Could the best day of her life really come so soon after the worst?

She ripped open the envelope, heart pounding with excitement. Then she read the first few lines — and slumped against the wall, the hollow feeling in the pit of her stomach threatening to swallow her whole.

Thank you for your interest in Princeton University. We regret to inform you . . .

It was as far as she got — but it was far enough.

"Everything all right?" Fiona suddenly appeared in the room, her face a mask of fake concern.

"I've been rejected from Princeton," Sam said, in a voice dead of emotion.

"Noooo. But you studied so hard."

Barely hearing her, Sam tore up the letter, letting the pieces fall through her fingers. "I can't believe I actually thought I had a chance," she murmured to herself. When would she ever learn? You couldn't expect things, hope for things. In the end, it just meant getting hurt.

"Sam, I am so, so, so sorry," Fiona said, her voice oozing with artificial distress. "God, life can be so unfair." She switched into her baby talk voice. "You want a cookie?"

That was it — she couldn't take any more. Sam raced upstairs to her attic, to hide from Princeton, from Fiona, from a world that seemed out to get her.

"Don't forget," Fiona called after her, "you have to work tonight!"

But Sam was already up the stairs. Safe. Slamming her door shut, she flung herself facedown onto her bed and burst into tears, crying, sobbing like she hadn't in years. Not since she was a little girl, and she'd lost the one thing that had made her life worth living. All she'd had left after that was hope — hope that someday, somehow, things would get better. And now she didn't even have that.

It wasn't fair, she fumed. She'd worked so hard, she'd lived through so much misery — and still, nothing worked out for her. Nothing!

She cried and cried until, chest heaving, her face soaked in tears, she lost the strength even for that. She was too tired, too drained — all the emotion had poured out of her, and now there was nothing left. Nothing but empti-ness.

Eyes red, she knelt on the floor and pulled out a dusty old footlocker from under her bed. She pulled it open, and began to sift through a lifetime of memories.

Blue ribbons.

Baseball cards.

A photo of her mom and dad, together, happy.

A newspaper clipping about the earthquake — the one that had taken him away.

"I miss you, Dad," she whispered. She closed her eyes, wishing that when she opened them, he would be standing there, ready to take her in his arms and comfort her the way he always used to do. Say exactly the right thing to make her feel better, to make her feel like everything would work out, like she could take on the world. She'd never wished for anything so hard in her life.

But of course, when she opened her eyes, the room was empty. He was never coming back.

She pulled out the last item in the box — her old book of fairy tales. The one they'd been reading together on that last night. When he'd promised her that life was a fairy tale, that it would have a happy ending. When he'd promised her that he would come back.

Suddenly angry, Sam hurled the book across the room. As the book slammed into the wall and fell to the floor, a folded paper slipped out from the back binding.

But Sam didn't notice. She climbed into bed and pulled the blanket up over her head, leaving the book where it lay. She was done with fairy tales. She didn't believe in happy endings anymore. She didn't believe in anything anymore.

♛　　♛　　♛

Days passed. Sam slogged through, minute by minute, hour by hour. Each moment seemed as colorless, as hopeless, as the last.

She spent her afternoons working in the diner, no longer minding the monotony — after all, she figured, this was her life. She'd better get used to it.

One afternoon, she knelt on her hands and knees, dutifully scrubbing the kitchen floor. It seemed about as low as a person could get. As she stood up, one of her roller skates skidded out from under her, almost knocking her to the ground. Sick and tired of them, of everything, Sam wearily pulled the skates off and dropped them to the floor. Then, barefoot and deflated, she began scrubbing a new spot.

"Sam, what are you doing?" Rhonda asked, as she came into the kitchen and spotted her favorite busgirl crouched on all fours.

"Trying to get this grime off the floor," Sam said.

"I meant, what are you doing with the rest of your life?" Rhonda asked. She walked over to Sam and pulled her up off the ground.

"I'm Diner Girl," Sam said, refusing to meet her eyes. "I'm doing what Diner Girl does."

"Baby, what has gotten into you?" Rhonda said, taking her by the shoulders and giving her an affectionate shake. "You can't even see that you're blessed. Look around you — you've got a whole family behind you."

Sam looked behind her, to see Eleanor and Bobby looking on with concern.

"We love you, sweetheart," Eleanor said.

"You're our little Sammy," Bobby added.

Sam turned back to Rhonda, who put her arm around Sam. "We have faith in you — now have faith in yourself."

It was a touching moment. And it was completely destroyed as Brianna and Gabriella barreled their way into the restaurant. They slammed the door behind them so hard that Fiona's Elvis clock, her prized possession, was knocked off the wall and fell to the floor. It shattered.

"Mom!" Gabriella called out. "Sam broke your Elvis clock!"

Sam looked up at the door, where the clock had hung, and saw the dusty, faded piece of paper that had been hidden behind it for so many years. The quotation her father had pinned up. His motto. Their motto.

"Nice going, Sam," Fiona snapped as she entered the diner. "That's coming out of your salary. And cover up those stupid words. This is a diner, not a fortune cookie."

Sam wasn't paying attention. She was staring at the quote, repeating it over and over to herself. "Never let the fear of striking out keep you from playing the game."

The words affected her like never before. She could almost hear her father's voice, could almost imagine he was standing there beside her, giving her strength.

"Sam, I'm on my way to my lipo consultation," Fiona continued. "They're going to remove some fat from Gabriella to smooth the wrinkles in my knees."

"Mother, not again," Gabriella protested in horror.

"Don't worry, Gabriella," Fiona said. "Mommy's doing you a favor. Besides, you're young, it'll grow back. Have a cupcake."

Angrily, Gabriella grabbed a cupcake from the counter and shoved it into her mouth. At least it kept her from talking.

Which is more than could be said for Fiona.

"I need you to clean the pool tonight —" she began.

Sam read her father's quote again. And something inside her changed.

"No!" she told Fiona. For the first time in eight years.

"I quit," she said, the words coming out before she had a chance to think. "I quit this job, I quit your family — and I'm moving out!"

"And just where do you think you're going to live?" Fiona asked in a cool voice.

Sam hadn't thought that far ahead, but before she had a chance to reconsider, Rhonda jumped in.

"With me!" she said, throwing her arms around Sam in a triumphant hug.

Fiona looked as if she'd been slapped in the face. "You can't just walk out of here," she sputtered.

"Watch me," Sam said. And, feeling stronger than she'd felt in a long time, she walked purposefully toward Fiona, who backed away.

"You can mess with your hair, your nose, your face, and whatever else you want," Sam told her angrily. "You can mess with my dad's diner. But you can't mess with me."

And she stormed out.

"Wait for me!" Rhonda called, heading for the door.

"Walk out that door and you're fired," Fiona warned.

"That won't be necessary," Rhonda responded with a grin. "'Cause I quit!" She advanced on Fiona, who backed away from the very large, very angry waitress. "You know what?" she asked, only inches from Fiona's face. "The only reason I *ever* stayed here was to look after that girl. But now that she's free of you, there's nothing stopping me from kicking your butt."

She feinted toward Fiona, who yelped in fear and dropped to her knees, hands flying up to cover her nose.

"No, not the face!" she cried.

Rhonda just shook her head in disgust. "You're not even worth it," she said, walking out the door.

Eleanor took a step forward. "I quit, too," she said, and followed Rhonda out of the diner.

"Me too," Bobby added as he walked out the door behind them.

One by one, the customers slowly began to follow their lead, leaving their food, and the diner, behind.

Soon the room was empty, except for Fiona and her daughters.

Fiona picked herself up off the floor and dusted herself off, without a word to either of them.

"Way to go, Mom!" Brianna gushed.

"Yeah, you showed them," Gabriella agreed.

Fiona glared daggers at her identically idiotic spawn. "Shut up," she said wearily. And walked out the door herself.

chapter fourteen

$\mathcal{R}$honda and Sam carried Sam's trunk into the apartment, laying it down carefully on the living room floor. The room was already filled with boxes holding the rest of Sam's stuff. She was officially free of Fiona.

"I think that's the last of it," Rhonda said, flopping down on the couch in exhaustion. "The sofa pulls out to a bed. You sure you'll be okay with it?"

"Are you kidding?" Sam asked. "Anything's better than living with Fiona."

"I'm starving," Rhonda said. "You up for some pizza?"

Sam's grin faded, and she suddenly looked grim. "I'm going to have to take a rain check," she said. "I've still got some unfinished business to attend to."

"Is this about the kid from the car wash?" Rhonda asked.

"Yeah."

"If you want my advice," Rhonda began. She leaned forward, and in a low voice, suggested, "Hit him where it hurts."

♛ ♛ ♛

Sam threw open the door to the locker room — the boys' locker room, but she didn't care. She barged in and strode down the aisle as the roomful of half-dressed guys scrambled to cover themselves. Sam didn't even notice. She only had eyes for one thing, one person. And there he was, getting suited up for the night's big game.

He spotted her, and his mouth dropped open. Speechless.

They remained silent and motionless for a long time as the room cleared out. They just stared at each other. And Sam just waited. She wasn't going to be the first to speak.

Finally, Austin found his nerve. "Look, Sam . . . I know you think I'm a —"

"Coward? Phony?" Sam suggested.

"Listen, before you rip my head off —"

Sam interrupted him. "Austin, I didn't come here to yell at you," she said calmly, almost kindly.

"You didn't?"

"I came here to tell you that I know what it feels like to be afraid to show who you are. I was," she admitted. "But I'm not anymore. The thing is, I really don't care what people think anymore. I have no job, and no family, and no money for college, but you know what? I believe in myself, and I know that things are going to be okay." She paused, frowning. "It's you I feel sorry for."

Austin stood up, quick to defend himself. "Hey, you don't understand the pressure I'm under," he protested. "My dad's got my life all worked out for me. I'm trapped. There's nothing I can do."

David stuck his head around the corner of the locker room. "Dude, five minutes," he called.

"I'm coming," Austin assured him. He turned back to Sam. "Can I call you later?"

Sam looked at him sadly, then shook her head. "I know that guy who sent those e-mails is somewhere down inside you, but I can't wait for him," she said. "Because waiting for you is like waiting for rain in this drought."

Sam started to walk out, then paused and turned back.

"I dropped my mask, Austin," she said. "I hope that one day, you can drop yours."

She walked out with her head held high.

♕ ♕ ♕

Sam wandered through the empty halls, going over and over the conversation in her mind. Had she done the right thing? Had she made a horrible mistake? Thrown away something that could have been — something?

She shook her head. No. She'd done what she had to do. And things would work out. She just wished that she didn't have to work them out on her own, as always.

That's when she spotted Carter, lingering at the end of the hallway.

"What are you doing here?" Sam asked.

"I thought you could use a friend," he said simply.

Sam gave him a warm hug. It was good to know there was at least one person in her life who would always be there when she needed him.

"Did you set him straight?" Carter asked.

"You bet," she said, grinning. "So, what are you doing tonight?"

"Aaah . . ." Carter hesitated. "I was actually thinking of going to the game. But, I understand if you don't want to go."

"Why wouldn't I?" Sam asked.

"Really? You'd go to the game?"

Sam shrugged. "If I don't go, I'll just feel a lot worse. I just want to let Austin and Shelby and the rest of them know that they didn't break me." Then she smiled at her best friend. "Besides, if I don't go, who else is going to explain the game to you?"

They linked arms and began walking down the hallway together. That's when Sam noticed Carter's outfit — funky shirt, comfortable pants, a definite look, but she couldn't quite place it.

"I like what you're wearing," she commented, surprised. "Who are you supposed to be today?"

"Myself," Carter answered.

"I think it's your best look."

chapter fifteen

$\mathcal{F}$ive minutes to game time, and the air was electric with anticipation. The marching band banged out an almost on-key version of the school fight song, the cheerleaders warmed up the crowd, and Sam and Carter found their seats, hoping that this evening would end more success-fully than their last encounter with the world of football.

Down on the field, Shelby leaped down from her spot atop the human pyramid, glowing with pride. This was going to be *her* night, she could feel it.

"Austin and I are almost back together," she informed Madison and Caitlyn, who, as always, pretended to care. "I mean, we haven't made it official or anything, but it's on."

She could hardly wait until the game was over so that she and her champion quarterback could ride off into the sunset.

And there he was — warming up on the side of the field . . . and looking just a bit shell-shocked. He gazed up into the stands and, spotting Sam, looked quickly away.

"This is the big one, Austin," his father reminded him. "Stay focused and win it, okay? Everyone's counting on you."

Austin just stared at him wordlessly. What was there left to say?

♛   ♛   ♛

The kickoff came and went. The players raced up and down the field. The crowd cheered. Time passed.

And in the stands, Sam tried to care about the game — and tried *not* to care about one of the players.

"Austin Ames is racing up the field," the announcer called. "He's at the fifty . . . the forty . . . the thirty . . . uh-oh!"

One of the Lancers finally caught up with Austin and, with a flying tackle, knocked him to the ground.

"And he's brought down at the twenty-two-yard line!" the announcer called. "Nine seconds left. Frogs are on the twenty-two-yard line and need one touchdown to win. It all comes down to one person: Austin Ames."

That's when it began.

The chanting.

"Austin! Austin! Austin!"

Sam tried, she really did — but she just couldn't take it anymore. The sound of his name surrounded her, his face swam in front of her mind's eye, and suddenly, she couldn't breathe.

"You know what, Carter?" she said, standing. "I thought I could handle this, but I really can't. I think I have to go."

"Come on, there's only nine seconds left," Carter protested. Then he realized what the crowd was screaming — and saw the look on Sam's face. Resigned, he waved her away. "I'll let you know how it ends."

♛   ♛   ♛

Out on the field, Austin leaned into the team huddle, planning their next and last move. He glanced over to the sidelines, where the coach was signaling a play. But then Austin looked past him, up into the stands, where he saw Sam rising to leave. He followed her progress through the crowd for a moment, then turned back to his team — the guys were all looking at him expectantly, waiting for him to call the play.

They were counting on him, he knew it. So was the coach. So was his father.

And yet —

He looked back up to the stands — she was almost through the crowd. Was he going to let her walk away from him again? Maybe for the last time?

Or was he going to take a chance?

Austin looked back at his team, then broke out of the huddle.

"Sorry, guys," he said, sprinting off the field without another word.

"Wait a minute," the announcer said, confused. "Something's wrong. Ames is leaving the field!"

Austin broke through his teammates on the sidelines and was about to chase after Sam when his father grabbed him by the arm.

"Austin, what are you doing?" he asked.

"I'm outta here," Austin said.

His father looked furious. "You're throwing away your future," he objected.

"No, Dad. I'm throwing away *your* future." Austin looked his father in the eye and, for the first time in a long time, spoke his mind. "This is the *real* me."

Realizing he was still holding the football, Austin tossed it off to Ryan, who was hovering on the sidelines. "It's in your hands, bro."

Ryan jogged out to the huddle, and Austin pushed his way through the crowd, oblivious to the voices — his father, his coach, his girlfriend, his school — begging him to stay. He was through listening to what other people wanted from him, what other people needed him to be. He knew who he was now — and he knew who he wanted to be with.

And there she was, just beyond the field, only an arm's length away.

Austin reached out to her, gently grabbed her shoulder. She whirled around, and seeing him, her eyes widened in disbelief.

"Austin, the game isn't over. What are you doing?"

Austin tenderly cupped her chin in his hand, and pulled her close.

"Something I should have done a long time ago."

It was Sam's first real kiss — and it was perfect.

The world whirled around her as everything — other than the electrifying touch of his lips on hers — faded away. Nestled in Austin's arms, she finally felt at home, at peace.

They were so lost in each other that it took them several minutes to notice the raindrops falling on their heads. After weeks of drought, the skies had opened up. They both looked up, and smiled.

"I'm sorry I waited for the rain," Austin whispered. And, gazing into her eyes, he leaned in to kiss her again.

Back on the field, Ryan sloshed through the mud into the end zone, scoring the game-winning touchdown. The bleachers erupted in cheers as the triumphant crowd went crazy. A legion of fans rushed the field, hoisting Ryan onto their shoulders — and knocking Shelby facedown into a mud puddle.

It was an ending Sam and Austin would have loved, but they were too busy to notice. They were lost in each other's arms, lost in their dreams — dreams that had finally come true.

epilogue

*A*fterward, Sam would never remember whether or not they won the game that day, or how long it rained, or what they'd said to each other out there, under the stars. All she could remember was that kiss, that perfect kiss. And after that kiss, it was like everything fell into place.

Remember that folded piece of paper that fell out of her fairy tale book? Sam found it while she was cleaning out her old room. It turned out to be her dad's will. He had told her that she'd find something important in that book and it turned out to be true. According to the will, the diner, the house — everything — belonged to her.

With the law on her side, Sam called in the authorities, and Fiona was charged with forgery, grand theft, and being a pain in the neck.

Speaking of forgery, Sam also found the *real* letter from Princeton — at the bottom of Fiona's garbage can.

But, after all was said and done, Sam decided to drop the charges and forgive her stepfamily. With a few conditions.

Fiona made a deal with the DA and is now working off her debt to society. You can usually find her on her hands and knees, scrubbing the floor of the diner. *Sam's* diner. Fiona now works under the watchful eye of Sam and her new partners — Rhonda, Eleanor, and Bobby — who are only too happy to keep her in line.

Even Brianna and Gabriella were able to pitch in, finally putting their synchronization skills to good use — on roller skates. They're happy enough in their busgirl outfits, skating in sync — kind of. Nine times out of ten, of course, the skating lasts about five minutes before they crash into each other and send the food flying.

And Austin? After a good heart-to-heart talk, Austin's dad finally saw the light. And, according to the brand-new sign hanging in front of Big Andy's Car Wash, all Princeton football fans now get one hundred percent off (but bear in mind, they reserve the right to discriminate against anyone from Harvard and Yale).

Carter, who may have deserved a happy ending most of all, finally got his commercial. It's the one for that new zit cream, "Believe." You've probably seen him standing in front of the mirror with his newly clear skin, saying his favorite words: "Anything is possible, if you just *believe.*"

Case in point — as a consequence of landing the commercial, Carter landed the girl. As soon as he became famous — or, at least, televised — Shelby was all over him.

Carter couldn't have cared less. He and Astrid are now pretty much joined at the hip — and Carter's never been happier.

As for Sam and Austin, well, after a whirlwind summer romance, they drove off into the sunset together, Princeton-bound, and lived happily ever after.

At least, for now. . . .

After all, they're only freshmen!